ALSO BY KATIE ZHAO

Winnie Zeng Unleashes a Legend

WINNIE ZENG
VANQUISHES A KING

BOOK 2

KATIE ZHAO

RANDOM HOUSE NEW YORK

Text copyright © 2023 by Katherine Zhao
Jacket art copyright © 2023 by Sher Rill Ng

All rights reserved. Published in the United States by
Random House Children's Books, a division of
Penguin Random House LLC, New York.

Random House and the colophon are registered trademarks of
Penguin Random House LLC.

Visit us on the Web! rhcbooks.com

Educators and librarians, for a variety of teaching tools, visit us at
RHTeachersLibrarians.com

Library of Congress Cataloging-in-Publication Data
Name: Zhao, Katie, author.
Title: Winnie Zeng vanquishes a king / Katie Zhao.
Description: First edition. | New York: Random House Children's Books, [2023] |
Series: Winnie Zeng; 2 | Summary: As the balance between the human and spirit realm becomes more fragile as Halloween aproaches, Winnie Zeng and her archnemesis and fellow member of the Shaman Task Force, David, must work with a new shaman to keep their town safe.
Identifiers: LCCN 2022022958 (print) | LCCN 2022022959 (ebook) |
ISBN 978-0-593-42661-6 (hardcover) | ISBN 978-0-593-42662-3 (lib. bdg.) |
ISBN 978-0-593-42664-7 (pbk.) | ISBN 978-0-593-42663-0 (ebook)
Subjects: CYAC: Good and evil—Fiction. | Spirits—Fiction. | Magic—Fiction. |
Chinese Americans—Fiction. | LCGFT: Novels.
Classification: LCC PZ7.1.Z513 Wg 2023 (print) | LCC PZ7.1.Z513 (ebook) |
DDC [Fic]—dc23

Printed in the United States of America
1st Printing
First Edition

Kitchen appliances and tools are not toys and should be used carefully. The activities described on pages 274–277 require cooking and should be performed under adult supervision and with an adult's permission.

For Penny

CHAPTER ONE

My name is Winnie Zeng, and if there's one piece of advice you should take from me, it's to never go to middle school, ever. Avoid it for as long as you can. Run away from home if you need to. Also, if you ever receive a pamphlet from something called the Shaman Task Force, sprint as fast as you can in the opposite direction, before a bunch of spirits start attacking your town and you're roped into never-ending patrol duty.

Okay, that was a lot. Let's back up a little.

See, up until the day I entered sixth grade, my daily life was pretty normal and boring. Going to school every day. Watching (and rewatching, and rewatching . . .) *Sailor Moon*. Bugging my fourteen-year-old sister, Lisa. Practicing the piano (or, rather, concocting schemes to trick my family into thinking I was practicing piano). Doing my best to one-up my archnemesis, a kid named David Zuo. You know, real average stuff. And it was *great*.

Then I got to sixth grade, and everything changed. Most kids hit puberty when they get to middle school, which is one of the many reasons why middle school drools. But instead of getting a growth spurt, I developed shaman powers.

Yeah, you read that right. *Shaman powers.*

Basically, that means I developed the ability to see spirits that have crossed over from the spirit realm into the human world. Apparently, these powers have been passed down in my family for generations. Some families pass down valuable heirlooms, or property, or wealth, but in the Zeng family, we get unwanted powers instead. Yay.

Not only that, but because I had these shaman powers, I got roped into joining the Shaman Task Force. Being a taskforce member means serving as a peacekeeper between the shaman and human worlds. It's a big responsibility to handle on top of my already-important middle school tasks. Hey, if I'm not going to annoy the heck out of my older sister, then who will?

Because it's so important that no evil spirits cause chaos in the human world, I can't mess up.

"Winnie, you messed up."

"Wh-what?" Startled, I stopped in the middle of what I was currently doing—beating eggs together to mix into flour.

The silvery, ghostly figure of my grandmother's spirit hovered over my shoulder, frowning down at the cookbook on the kitchen counter, which was open to the recipe for sugar cookies. It was one of the easiest types of cookies to make, and after an extremely hectic few weeks, all I wanted was to make something very simple. And nonmagical.

"You added only half the amount of flour you were supposed to," chided Lao Lao. My grandmother was a shaman before me, but she died before I was born, so I never got to know her when she was alive. Up until several weeks ago, I didn't have an inkling that I would ever get to meet Lao Lao in any form.

Then I discovered my grandmother's magical cookbook and unleashed her spirit. After a whole lot of confusion, she became an overspirit—*my* overspirit. Shamans are pretty much useless without our overspirits to guide us. Well, not completely useless, but we are much more powerful when we have our overspirits by our sides. The catch is that Lao Lao is anchored to my pet rabbit, Jade, which means I have to haul around a rabbit everywhere if I want my overspirit's guidance. That made for one very hectic afternoon at Chinese school, in which the principal lost her head over me bringing a "rat" to class (long story).

With Lao Lao's aid, I'm able to use magic to protect the human world from spirits, or so it's supposed to go. By accessing my grandmother's magic—a process called *combining*—I managed to vanquish the rogue spirit of Hou Yi back during the Mid-Autumn Festival. Supposedly with more training, I'll develop my powers to the level of being able to do this regularly. But so far having my grandmother as my overspirit really means that I get lectured 24-7.

I glanced down at the recipe and groaned when I realized my grandmother was right. "Well, at least it's an easy fix." I scooped out another cup of flour and added it to the mixing bowl.

"You need more attention to detail, Winnie," my grandmother scolded. "What if a rogue spirit were right under your nose, and you didn't even notice?"

"You can't compare baking cookies to capturing spirits," I protested.

Lao Lao harrumphed, turning her nose up into the air. "I hope you work on your attitude, too, before we go to meet the Spirit Council tomorrow morning."

The Spirit Council is the governing body of the Shaman Task Force. I'd never met the Spirit Council members before, but I'd heard all about them. After I successfully captured the spirit of Hou Yi and saved Groton, they'd summoned me to officially appoint me as a member of the Shaman Task Force. Though I'd never met the mysterious Spirit Council, my grandmother had told me enough about them that I knew they were a big deal—and that it was a big deal to meet them. They seemed to oversee the operations of shamans in the human world, specifically the members of the Shaman Task Force, who keep evil spirits out of Earth.

"Did you hear me, Winnie? You'll have to be on your best behavior to make a good impression on the Spirit Council."

"I got it, Lao Lao," I sighed. I was trying to relax by baking these cookies, and she was totally killing the mood.

"Hmph. You're not taking this seriously enough. Why,

when I met the council for the first time, I bought a new dress and ..."

My grandmother kept rambling, but I tuned her out and finished baking the cookies. It was easy enough to pretend I was listening by throwing in a "you're right" or an "absolutely" here and there. When the cookies were finished, I let them cool for a bit before biting into one.

"How is it?" Lao Lao asked, looking at the cookies somewhat wistfully. Now that she was a spirit, she couldn't taste nonmagical human food. She'd been a renowned chef when she was alive, so I knew it had to be torturous watching me eat food all the time.

I smiled. "Absolutely *delicious.*"

The next morning, a little before ten, I dressed in my nicest pink sundress, black cardigan, and black flats.

"You look nice," Lao Lao said approvingly from behind me as I stared at myself in the mirror.

"I look like I'm going to a piano recital," I grumbled.

When I walked downstairs into the kitchen, my sister, Lisa, was sitting there eating her usual breakfast—a bowl of sugary cereal. She glanced up and did a double take. "Whoa. What's the occasion?" She was dressed in her typical gym attire, which meant Lululemon from head to foot.

"There's no occasion," I said as I grabbed a granola bar from the pantry. "I don't look any different from usual."

"Yes, you do. Usually you look like something the cat dragged in."

"Thanks. Well, if you have to know, today I have a very important meeting with the all-important Spirit Council to discuss how I'm going to use my superpowers to save the world from a bunch of evil spirits."

"Fine. Don't tell me what you're doing, then." Lisa rolled her eyes. "Where do you even come up with such ridiculous stuff to say?"

As I rummaged through the fridge, looking for the milk, Lao Lao hissed angrily, "Winnie, you can't just reveal highly confidential information like that! It's very important that humans don't find out about the existence of shamans and spirits, good or bad. Otherwise they'll panic and no doubt ruin everything by trying to keep the peace on their own."

"Relax," I muttered under my breath. "I only said that 'cause I knew Lisa wouldn't even believe me." My older sister was so oblivious to the supernatural disturbances in our town that she hadn't even noticed when her then-boyfriend Matt was possessed by an evil spirit.

My grandmother must have grown tired of lecturing me, because she just sighed and shook her head.

"Oh, tell Mama and Baba that I'm going to study at the Suntreader, if they ask," I called over my shoulder to Lisa as I opened the front door.

It was a sunny morning in Groton, the perfect day to bike to the local bookstore, the Suntreader. After greeting the owner, Mr. Stevens, I made my way through the crowd of people browsing the bookshelves. I soon found myself standing in front of a magical elevator.

A new button had appeared above the one marked 88—the button that would take me to the eight hundred and eighty-eighth floor. Yup, you heard me right, the *eight hundred and eighty-eighth floor.* Though, technically, no regular mortals could access this floor. Only supernatural beings and powerful humans who could see them—a.k.a. shamans.

I certainly didn't feel like a powerful shaman. My stomach swooped with nerves. What if the Spirit Council didn't like me? Worse, what if they liked me *too* much and decided I'd be in charge of every spirit-capturing task from now on? I couldn't decide which would be worse.

"Oh, I didn't mention this before, but I can't go in with you. You have to go greet the Spirit Council on your own," Lao Lao said gently.

"R-really?" Oh boy. My stomach was tying itself into knots. Nervous didn't even begin to describe what I was feeling. This was worse than that one time I had to perform at a piano recital and just completely forgot the opening notes seconds before I went up onstage.

Yet amid my nerves there was a certain amount of excitement as well. Once I met the Spirit Council, I'd be taking another huge step forward in my progress as a shaman. No matter what happened, my life was about to take a drastic turn—yet again. "You sure you can't come with me, Lao Lao?"

My grandmother shook her head solemnly. "Not for

this first meeting. The Spirit Council has requested to meet with you, and only you."

"What if I get lost?" *What if I'm extremely awkward, and the Spirit Council thinks I'm weird and immediately decides I'm not fit to be a member of the Shaman Task Force?*

"Impossible," Lao Lao scoffed. "You'll see the Spirit Council immediately when you walk in. Can't possibly miss them."

"You're underestimating my poor sense of direction. Sometimes I still get lost in our neighborhood." In my defense, my neighborhood is huge, and Google Maps is always sending me off in the wrong direction. "Why *can't* you come inside with me, Lao Lao?"

"Not for your initiation into the Shaman Task Force. The Spirit Council operates by its own rules," she said vaguely.

Whatever that meant. Grown-ups never make any sense. Especially not the immortal, magical, all-knowing kind of grown-ups.

Taking a deep breath, I stepped into the elevator and flashed Lao Lao one last reassuring grin. I reminded myself of the reasons I deserved to be here. *You just brought down the powerful spirit of the legendary archer Hou Yi. You can definitely do something as simple as greet the Spirit Council on your own,* I told myself. Somehow, though, the idea of going for round two with Hou Yi was more appealing than finally meeting the mysterious and all-knowing Spirit Council.

The elevator shot up again, this time much faster than

before. My ears popped the way they did sometimes when I was flying in an airplane. After what felt like ages, the elevator ground to a halt, and my stomach dropped again. If I made it back down in the elevator without tossing my cookies, it would be a miracle.

The doors opened. An invisible force flung me forward, as though the elevator were ejecting me rather rudely. "Oof!" I landed on all fours on a soft, fluffy surface.

When I dared to open my eyes, I found that I was surrounded by whiteness, and that the fluffy surface I'd landed on was a cloud.

Well, one thing was certain: I definitely wasn't in Kansas anymore. Or Michigan. Or the United States. Maybe that elevator had launched me straight up into outer space.

I probably would've been more shocked to find myself somehow among the clouds if the past weeks hadn't been filled with me discovering that spirits were real. Oh, and that I was supposed to be a shaman, keeping the peace between the human and spirit realms. Yeah, how's *that* for a rude awakening? Nothing could faze me now, except maybe David becoming not annoying.

"H-hello?" Slowly, I stood up and gazed around me. Tall white pillars loomed out of the endless clouds. It looked like I was in a temple in the clouds—a temple that was made *out* of clouds. Clouds that somehow felt solid beneath my feet.

As the clouds parted, I narrowed my eyes and realized that there were gray stone statues between the pillars looming out of the white mist. They were shaped like animals.

A rat. A boar. A dragon. A rooster. I counted twelve in total, and it took me a few seconds to realize what they were.

"It's . . . the animals of the zodiac," I gasped. I'd learned about them in Chinese school and seen them on those disposable paper place mats in Chinese restaurants.

"You're correct, Zeng Weini," rumbled a low, unfamiliar voice.

CHAPTER TWO

I hadn't realized I wasn't alone. Turning around, I saw a man with long white hair and a beard emerge from behind the rooster statue. In fact, several figures appeared from behind the zodiac statutes. They wore gray robes with long, billowing sleeves. Their hands were clasped together, as though in prayer.

My heart hammered. "You—you're—?"

"We're the guardians of the Spirit Council," explained the man with long white hair. "I'm the grand master, Jizha. It's good to finally meet you in person, Weini—or, you prefer to go by the name Winnie, correct?"

I gaped as Jizha's words registered. In person? Had we met *not* in person before? I was pretty sure we hadn't. I would've remembered these people for sure.

One by one, the other Spirit Council members stepped forward from their statues. Though there were twelve in total, only three stood at the very front. Jizha was in the middle, flanked by two women. The taller one, who stood in front of the boar statue, introduced herself as Zhula, while the shorter one in front of the tiger statue said her name was Huna.

"We may not have met formally, but rest assured that we know all about you, Winnie," said Huna.

That sounded ominous. I did not rest assured.

"We, the Spirit Council, have been watching over you from afar," Jizha explained, correctly interpreting the confusion on my face. "We've been impressed with your accomplishments. Of course, it was evident—to me, at least—that you would be a very capable shaman. Your grandmother's blood runs through your veins, after all."

"Your grandmother Wang Yipei. One of the finest shamans we ever had," added the woman who stood in front of the dragon statue.

It took me a moment to recognize my grandmother's name, because in my family we'd always referred to her as Lao Lao. "Y-yeah." I tried to force the stutter out of my voice, without much luck. I was probably making a *super* first impression.

"So you changed your mind, then, Weini?" asked Zhula. Her tone sounded much harsher than the others. "Didn't you decide at one point to revoke any shaman responsibility?"

All eyes watched me, some with curiosity, some with accusation. The woman was right, though. At first I hadn't taken my shaman responsibility seriously, hadn't even wanted it—that is, until the Mid-Autumn Festival, when I'd stepped in to save my town from a rampaging spirit.

Now I *did* want to take this shaman business seriously,

but maybe it was too late. "I . . . I changed my mind. I *do* want to be part of the Shaman Task Force and help protect the human world."

"Changed your mind." Zhula snorted. "What if you change your mind again, mid-battle? What use does the Spirit Council have for a wishy-washy shaman?"

Wishy-washy. I cringed at the word, the tips of my ears heating from embarrassment, but it wasn't like Zhula was wrong to tell me off. I *had* been wishy-washy in the past, until I'd realized that protecting Groton from evil was just as important as—no, *more* important than—getting good grades or one-upping David. Plus, I couldn't deny that there was something really cool about having special powers and being a secret hero in Groton. Knowing that there was something only *I* could do. Now that I'd set my mind to honing my shaman abilities, I was going to be the best shaman out there.

"That's enough, Zhula," Huna said quietly, but Zhula either didn't hear her or pretended not to.

"Sure, you might have succeeded in capturing the spirit of Hou Yi, but that could be a fluke." Zhula was clearly on the verge of saying more, but she finally held her tongue when Jizha raised his hand.

My cheeks burned. I wanted to say something in my defense, but that would probably only make things worse. Zhula seemed determined to dislike me, no matter what. With that glower on her face, she could even give Lisa a run for her money.

Jizha frowned at Zhula. "We should believe in Winnie and her abilities. And we should have confidence that she won't change her mind again or, as you put it, be *wishy-washy*. We need Winnie's help, after all." There was an ominous undertone to his voice that made me a bit nervous. Why did the Spirit Council *need* me? Zhula said nothing, just huffed and turned her head to the side.

"I'm sorry," I blurted. "It's just—I had a lot on my plate, between homework, and a piano recital, and . . ." My voice trailed off when no sympathy rose on the council members' stony faces. I mean, what had I expected? *Oh, of course, Winnie, we understand that finishing book reports comes before saving the world?* Something told me the Spirit Council members wouldn't recognize an SAT workbook if it danced naked in front of them. Probably didn't even know what a piano recital was. Lucky them. "I . . . I was being selfish before." It wasn't easy admitting that to myself, let alone to the Spirit Council. "But I'm ready now. I want to be the one to protect my town from evil."

The other council members looked toward Jizha, who examined me with a face empty of expression. "Being a member of the Shaman Task Force is a huge responsibility," Jizha said. "Your grandmother bore it before you, and she had to make many sacrifices to attend to her duties. It's the most important job you'll ever have in your life, little one. Once you've decided to take it on, there is no quitting."

My parents would probably argue that my future career

as a doctor-lawyer-engineer was far more important, but I decided that now wasn't the time to point that out.

"I understand," I said, trying to sound more confident than I felt.

"You've proven that you're capable of stepping up to the task. You unlocked True Sight once, successfully combining your powers with your overspirit's in order to decipher the True Name of an evil spirit. But that is only the beginning of your journey as a shaman."

"In the past, shamans have managed to fumble their way into using True Sight," Zhula said snidely.

"Those cases were the exception," countered Huna, which earned her a glare from Zhula. "The overwhelming majority of our shamans have only been able to use True Sight after much training."

This seemed to be true, because Zhula fell silent for a moment. Finally, she sniffed and said, "Still, my point is that Winnie has yet to *really* prove herself. The ultimate test of a shaman's prowess is being able to use True Sight at will."

My smile fell a little. Of course I'd known that using True Sight once didn't mean I was an exceptional shaman or anything, but Zhula was making it sound like I really had my work cut out for me.

"Winnie still has much more training to undergo, but she has achieved something impressive already. Can we agree on that?" Jizha asked.

Nobody had anything to say, but several council members nodded, which I guessed was confirmation that I was doing all right as a shaman so far.

He turned toward me and continued, "Your next goal as a shaman, should you continue pursuing this path, will be to master True Sight, until it feels as natural as breathing. Are you willing wholeheartedly to continue your training and dedicate yourself to the Shaman Task Force, Zeng Weini?"

Other than Zhula, who wore a skeptical expression, the council members gave me nods and smiles. I knew they meant to encourage me, but my stomach squirmed with uncertainty.

Was I ready? If I was honest with myself, I was pretty sure I'd never been less ready for anything in my whole life. Including that one time I played at my piano recital after only sleeping two hours the night before, which resulted in me forgetting half my music while onstage—not one of my finer moments.

But something told me this was a test. I had to at least *try* to appear ready. Put on a brave face for the Spirit Council, for Lao Lao, and for the world. Life was about to get a whole lot busier, because I planned to keep doing my best to make my family proud of me, as well as the Spirit Council. But I was up for the task.

"I'm ready to use my shaman powers for good. I promise. *Pinkie* promise." I held out my pinkie to show how serious I was.

Huna gave me the tiniest of smiles. Jizha's expression

didn't change. Zhula snorted, but everyone else gave me encouraging nods.

"Good. Then you must swear the Shaman Task Force oath. Listen to me carefully." Jizha cleared his throat, and when he spoke again, his words sounded louder, much more enunciated. "I, Winnie Zeng, am a member of the Shaman Task Force. I swear to protect the human world from supernatural forces to the best of my ability, until my dying breath."

Dying breath? That sounded dangerous. A small part of me wanted to protest, but a larger part of me recognized that I'd come too far to go back, no matter what. And I'd always known that I'd be risking my life by swearing to protect humans from evil spirits.

I was so busy worrying that it took me a moment to realize the Spirit Council members were all staring at me expectantly.

"Oh . . . sorry, can you repeat the oath?" I asked.

Jizha looked annoyed but did so. This time, I repeated it back to him. Once I finished speaking, I half expected to be enveloped in magic dust or grow twenty feet taller to indicate that something very cool had happened. But nothing changed. A bit disappointing.

Jizha waved one of his giant sleeves. Out of thin air, a black badge appeared on my shirt, right over my heart. "Whoa!" I gasped. The gold lettering on the badge read WINNIE ZENG, ROOKIE AGENT, SHAMAN TASK FORCE. And, in smaller print beneath that: GROTON BRANCH. I reached out and touched it. It was made out of leather and felt like a normal badge.

"'Rookie agent'?" I said, reading the text.

"That's your current title," explained Zhula. "Every shaman on our task force starts out as a rookie. Then you'll advance to level one, level two, level three—and, hopefully, up to level five, the final level. To get to level one, you'll need to capture fifty spirits, or successfully complete an emergency task."

I tried to picture myself fulfilling either of those requirements and got exhausted just thinking about it. *Fifty* spirits?

"This badge serves as both a mark of your commitment and a communication device," explained Huna. "Only shamans and spirits can see the badges. You don't have to remember to take them off when you change shirts, because they automatically transfer to the new shirt."

That was good to hear, because I definitely would have forgotten to take off the badge, and it would have ended up in the laundry.

"When the Spirit Council requires your services, we'll notify you," continued Huna. "The badge will glow, and you'll know to come to the headquarters of the Spirit Council."

"Oh." I nodded, but inside I was wondering just how frequently the council would be summoning me. What if they called in the middle of class? Teachers weren't all that understanding about their students leaving class without a legitimate excuse, and somehow I didn't think *answering the summons of a mysterious spirit council* counted as a legitimate excuse.

A small, thin smile rose to Jizha's lips, as though he knew exactly what I was thinking. "Don't worry. We won't call you that often."

I let out a nervous laugh. "Thank you."

"And vice versa—you can use the badge to communicate with us anytime you need." Jizha inclined his head toward me.

"Maybe not *any*time," muttered another council member. "We're busy people, you know."

"You sleep eighteen hours a day," said Zhula, rolling her eyes.

"Being a Spirit Council member is hard work! I need my eighteen hours of beauty rest!"

I pressed my fingers to my shiny new badge, still marveling over it. Even though the Spirit Council had sworn me in as a rookie agent, with this badge as evidence, I didn't feel like I'd accomplished enough yet to earn that title. They were putting an awful lot of trust in someone who occasionally went to school with her shirt inside out.

Even though I didn't feel worthy of wearing this badge just yet, at that moment I promised that I *would* be. I'd show everyone—including myself—that the Spirit Council was right to put their trust in me to help keep the peace between the spirit and human worlds. That was a promise.

"Now, are you ready for your first task?" Jizha asked.

I took a deep breath and nodded.

Jizha smiled. "Great. We've received intelligence that there is a class three spirit on the loose somewhere in Groton. More specifically, it has been moving back and forth between the spirit and human worlds, likely through the use of a hidden portal, indicating that it is a particularly clever and powerful evil spirit."

Clever and powerful and evil. Just what Groton needed. "Um . . . do you have any other information on this spirit?" I asked.

Jizha shook his head. "Not at the moment, I'm afraid. We're counting on you to capture this rogue spirit and send it back to the spirit realm."

I nodded as if I had any idea how I might accomplish that. I was going to have a *lot* of questions for Lao Lao later. Like it or not, I was now an official member of the Shaman Task Force. I had to capture this spirit before it caused chaos in my town. The last time a class three spirit—Hou Yi—had roamed free in Groton, it had brought about *way* too much mayhem.

"I'll do my best," I said, trying to sound as confident as I had earlier.

"In general, you should stay on alert, agent," said Zhula. For once, it seemed she was sincerely trying to be helpful. "With Halloween around the corner, there is a high likelihood that chaotic spirits will be more active. . . ." Zhula glanced over at the man standing in front of the snake statue, who grimaced at her.

"What?" I said, feeling like I was missing something.

"Well, we've sensed higher levels of spirit activity in the spirit realm," Jizha interjected. "As rogue spirits are drawn to shamans, this means you should always be ready to protect yourself—and those around you—at a moment's notice. At least until spirit activity has decreased once more."

Great.

"If we do require your assistance handling anything particularly nasty in addition to this class three spirit, we will be in contact." Jizha tapped the spot on his chest where my badge sat on mine.

I managed a small smile, even though my stomach was churning with nerves. I'd just had to deal with spirits that emerged during the Mid-Autumn Festival, and now they were going to surge during Halloween, too? Did spirits not take any vacations from being evil around the holidays?

Well, on the bright side, at least I'd have plenty of opportunities to capture spirits and prove myself worthy of my Shaman Task Force badge.

The Spirit Council members inclined their heads to me. I understood that to mean I was officially dismissed.

Still marveling over my badge, I headed back to the elevator and went all the way down to the first floor. Lao Lao was waiting for me with an anxious look on her face.

"How did it go?" she asked, rushing toward me. Apparently, Lao Lao had been worried, too, even though she hadn't seemed so earlier.

I flashed my badge at her and grinned, trying to look

more confident than I felt. "It's official. You're looking at the newest Shaman Task Force member."

My grandmother's face broke out into a huge smile. "Even Zhula didn't give you a hard time?"

"Oh, she did," I said, my smile fading. "Is she—um—always like that?"

"Zhula was a cranky old bat when I was your age, too," Lao Lao sighed. "Some things never change."

"She didn't like you, either?"

"Nope." Lao Lao shrugged, and then winked at me. "But I turned out to be one of the best shamans they've ever had. That just means that whoever Zhula doesn't like will go on to do great things, right?"

I guessed that was one way to look at it. Feeling slightly cheered, I nodded. But my cheeriness quickly disappeared again when I remembered the mission the Spirit Council had given me moments ago. "Oh, and the council members gave me a task. There's a class three spirit loose in Groton, and I have to capture it. You wouldn't happen to have noticed anything . . . out of the ordinary lately, would you?"

Lao Lao's slight smile faded, and she wrinkled her eyebrows. "No, I haven't. They didn't give you further details about this spirit?"

"No, but I wish they had," I sighed. "Though they did tell me that I can use my badge to call them if I need help." I had a feeling I was going to be doing that a lot. The Spirit Council would probably soon regret giving me that option.

"Hmm. We won't let our guard down. We'll capture this

spirit, wherever and whatever it is," my grandmother reassured me. "Now come. Let's go home and eat those sugar cookies."

Already drooling at the thought, I followed my grandmother's spirit home.

CHAPTER THREE

It was early October, and fall was now in full swing in Groton. Everywhere I turned, someone was holding a Starbucks Pumpkin Spice Latte. The people in my neighborhood had put up spooky Halloween decorations, in their annual unofficial competition of having the most extravagantly decorated house. (Usually the winners were Mr. and Mrs. Spritz, because they buried their place in so many cobwebs and lights and pumpkins that you could hardly see the house underneath. Those people took this decoration business *seriously*.)

Mrs. Payton probably could've given the Spritzes a run for their money. Even though Halloween was still a few weeks away, my homeroom teacher had pulled out all the stops to decorate her classroom. Orange and black paper streamers were strung up on the ceiling, orange lights lined the walls, and there was a smiling green jack-o'-lantern on her desk.

"I love your decorations, Mrs. Payton," Jeremy said loudly.

The bell hadn't even rung yet to signal the start of class,

and Jeremy was already trying to score extra brownie points with our teacher. It figured. That kid was always sucking up.

"Thank you. I got them on sale last year at Costco. Fifty percent off!" Mrs. Payton beamed.

The bell rang moments later, and Kim dashed through the door at record speed. Our teacher wasted no time getting class started. "Kim, please shut the door behind you. Jeremy, will you kindly pass out these flyers, please?" Mrs. Payton asked, indicating the large stack of pink papers beside her jack-o'-lantern.

"Next week, the sixth graders will be taking a field trip to the Museum of Art History," Mrs. Payton explained. "If you'd like to participate, I'll need your parent or guardian to sign this permission slip. Mr. Burnside and I are also looking for a handful of chaperones, so there's a place on the permission slip for your parent or guardian to volunteer as well."

Okay, so I wasn't the biggest fan of museums, but I was definitely a big fan of getting out of class. According to the permission slip, the sixth graders would be away from school for an *entire* day.

That was all the motivation I needed to go.

At dinner that evening, it was just my mother and me. Baba was still at work, as usual, and Lisa was at some evening study group. It was a peaceful evening in the Zeng household. I'd spent the afternoon practicing meditation with Lao Lao, which she'd insisted on incorporating into our regular training routine. Meditation was supposed to help me refine my focus. It was really boring, but if I wanted to become a capable shaman, I had to listen to my grandmother.

"Mama, will you sign this field-trip permission slip for me?" I asked out of the blue.

"Field trip?" Mama glanced up from her plate, eyebrows scrunching together in suspicion. "What field trip?"

I pulled out the permission slip with some hesitation. Though I was pretty sure I could get my mother to *eventually* agree to letting me go on the field trip, it would probably take some convincing on my part to get us there. My mother could be overprotective sometimes. She didn't even let me go to sleepovers at friends' houses.

Mama held out her hand, a slight frown on her face. I handed over the permission slip and waited with bated breath as she read it over. I sensed a volley of questions coming my way, and sure enough, Mama began firing them off like nobody's business. "Who else is going on this field trip? How will you make up for missing a full day of school?"

"*Everyone* is going, Mama," I said. "And I don't need to make up for this, because we'll still be learning at the museum."

"How will you get there?"

"Bus."

"What will you eat that day?"

"Food."

"What if you get injured? Who will look out for you?"

"Getting injured at a *museum?*" I scoffed. "Unlikely. The teachers and chaperones are going to look after us."

Mama opened and closed her mouth, but no words came out. At long last, she sighed and shook her head, which I recognized as her acceptance of defeat. *Yes.* "We'll talk about this when your father gets home."

"What? But Baba doesn't get home until much later," I complained.

"Not tonight. He'll be back early. In fact, your father should be home any— Ah!" Mama's words were cut off by the loud, rumbling noise that I recognized as the garage door opening.

A couple minutes later, Baba came through the back door, dressed in his fancy black business suit that he wore at his fancy law firm. My father's face was weathered with exhaustion. He dropped his briefcase on the kitchen island and said, "What's for dinner?"

"Baba, can you sign my field-trip permission slip?" I blurted out.

"Your what?"

After I caught Baba up to speed, I held my breath, hoping for a yes. He surprised me by immediately agreeing. Maybe he was just too tired to argue. While Mama still didn't look completely convinced, Baba got the final word around here, so she had no choice but to watch as he read the slip.

"Next Wednesday . . . ," Baba muttered to himself. "I can volunteer for your trip, too."

"You can?" I said, surprised.

"Yes. Next week's workload will be light, and my boss has been telling me to make better use of my paid time off," Baba said.

My insides warmed with happiness as I watched my father write his name in the volunteer slot. Even though I was trying not to make a big deal out of this, it *was* totally a big deal. Baba was always at his office. If he spent any more time there, they were going to start charging him rent. I couldn't remember the last time we'd spent a decent chunk of time together, and he'd never volunteered to do anything for my school before.

The sixth-grade field trip was shaping up to be pretty awesome.

The closer we got to Halloween, the more my excitement grew, especially as I thought of all the candy I was going to eat in a matter of weeks. But when I remembered the Spirit Council's warnings about increased spirit activity during Halloween, my mood would plummet again.

Still, spirits or not, Halloween was one of my favorite holidays. I mean, when else do you get an excuse to eat a bunch of candy and dress up however you want? Plus, everyone is in a good mood in the days leading up to

Halloween. It's impossible not to be. Nobody can hate Halloween.

"I hate Halloween," declared David as we were biking back from school, headed toward my house.

Okay, correction. Nobody *rational* can hate Halloween.

I jerked my handlebar too quickly and narrowly avoided pedaling into a tree. "You what?"

"I said I hate Halloween," he repeated. "What a silly, pointless holiday."

"Of course there is a point. The point of Halloween is to eat candy!" This was very common knowledge. I couldn't believe what I was hearing.

"I don't like candy. It's too sweet, and it's bad for my teeth."

If I needed any further proof to solidify my theory that David was a forty-year-old trapped in a twelve-year-old's body, this was it. Nobody under the age of twenty could hate candy. It was biology or something.

David has always been mature for his age. Or, at least, he's masterful at acting mature when adults are around. When they aren't looking, though? David turns into the most annoying kid ever. For the longest time, we competed against each other in everything from piano competitions to Chinese school tests. Now that David and I attended Groton Middle School together and had discovered that we were both shamans, the competition had intensified. Though, thanks to the fact that we had teamed up to capture the rogue spirit of Hou Yi, I was beginning to learn that he wasn't *that* bad all the time. Don't tell him I said that, though.

"You're weird," I said, which wasn't one of my finer comebacks, but in my defense, I was still very thrown.

David stuck his tongue out at me. See? Poster child for immature.

Over David's shoulder, there was the spirit of his ancestor, an old man with a long white beard who was dressed in elegant red-and-gold robes. A former Chinese emperor who now went by the name . . . Joe. Yeah, I know, an emperor named Joe. I couldn't even make that up if I tried. Joe is David's overspirit, like Lao Lao is mine.

"You're both weird," said Joe.

"Shut up, Joe," we replied in unison. At least David and I could agree on the important things.

"That's very rude," sniffed the former emperor. "I could have had your heads for such an insult back in the days of my reign! My servants would have put you in your place in an instant." He snapped his fingers.

"That was a long time ago," I shot back. "All your servants are dust now."

Joe shook his finger at me, his cheeks darkening with anger. Too bad I didn't get any shaman points for winning arguments with Joe, otherwise I'd easily be a level ten agent by the end of the day. "You—you youngsters have no manners these days! Oh, the trouble you'd be in if this were the Ming dynasty . . ." He continued his lecture, but I couldn't hear the rest, because I sped up my pedaling to put more distance between us.

"Hey, Winnie, wait up!" David shouted. In moments he'd pedaled so fast that his bike was parallel to mine. "I wanted to talk to you about something." He lowered his voice, making him sound suddenly serious. "You've met with the Spirit Council to get officially sworn in as a Shaman Task Force member, right?"

"Yeah. They even gave me a mission—to capture this class three spirit that's currently loose in Groton. I haven't gotten any leads yet, though." I flashed back to my tense and eventful meeting with the Spirit Council. Though it hadn't been all sunshine and rainbows, I'd emerged from that meeting with an official badge, not to mention a strengthened sense of purpose as a rookie agent. So, all in all, meeting the Spirit Council had gone about as well as I could've hoped for. "You met with them, too?"

David nodded, though his expression remained just as grim. You'd think someone had told him school was canceled forever or something. He unzipped his navy-blue bomber jacket, moving it aside to show me the black shaman badge on his shirt. "The Spirit Council told me about that class three spirit, too. But Joe and I haven't been able to sense anything. I'm kind of worried," David confided. "The Spirit Council mentioned that around Halloween, evil spirits will grow stronger in power. Sounds like we won't be getting a break."

I'd managed to forget that piece of information for all of ten minutes, but of course David had to remind me once again about how our lives were going to be *no* fun from now on. "These freaking spirits are always growing stronger," I grumbled. Seriously, weren't there other hobbies for them to take up in the spirit realm—tennis, knitting, underwater basket-weaving? "At this rate, you and I are never gonna get a vacation ever again." Jokes aside, it was also seriously concerning that we'd have to continue dealing with evil spirits in the lead-up to Halloween.

"Of course we can't live like we did before we discovered our powers," David said, sounding exasperated. "We're members of the Shaman Task Force now. We even swore oaths. Only death can prevent us from carrying out our mission."

As if I could've forgotten those details. "Yes, I am aware, David."

"Are you?" he scoffed. "Because you've seemed awfully chill about this whole thing. You didn't even want this responsibility in the beginning."

Even though I was pretty sure he hadn't meant them to, David's words stung. What did he mean by *awfully chill?* Did he think I didn't care enough about protecting the people of Groton? "Sorry for being so *chill.* What am I supposed to do, run around panicking like you?"

"I am not panicking."

I pointed over his shoulder and yelled, "Spirit!"

"AHHHHHH!" David screamed, and nearly fell off his

bike as he turned around to look. Point proven. When he realized there was nothing there and turned back toward me, the glare in his eyes could have melted steel. I couldn't resist snorting, which only caused his frown to deepen. "What is your problem, Winnie? Can't you take serious matters seriously for once?"

"I *am* taking this seriously," I insisted. "This is how I cope with stress, okay?"

"By making fun of me?"

"Yes!"

Truthfully, I'd been on edge ever since my meeting with the Spirit Council. It was an honor to work for the council, I knew. But it was also a huge responsibility. Sometimes I questioned how I'd stumbled my way into the task.

"You're so . . ." David rolled his eyes all the way up to the sky. I sensed he was holding back what he really wanted to say. "Whatever. Let's talk about something else. You excited for the class field trip tomorrow?"

"Oh, sure," I said, grateful for the sudden change of topic. Even though nothing about the Museum of Art History itself was all that exciting, I was looking forward to the field trip for two reasons. One, getting out of school for an entire day. And two, hanging out with Baba. I puffed out my chest. "My dad is going to be chaperoning. You'd better be on your best behavior, David."

"What do you mean? Of course I'll be on my best behavior, whether or not your dad is there," David protested. "I'm looking forward to our field trip way more than Halloween."

"Of course you are," I muttered under my breath.

David, oblivious, continued. "I already did some of my own research into the Museum of Art History, and I discovered . . ."

I'd already mastered the art of Tuning David Out—nodding and saying "Oh, that's cool" at frequent intervals—so I did that for the rest of the ride home.

When we got to my house, I immediately bounded up the stairs and headed for my room, while David stayed downstairs. Nobody else was home. Mama and Baba were both at work, and Lisa had after-school tutoring. Well, I guess there was *one* person—or, rather, spirit—home.

In the corner of my room was a small cage where my white rabbit, Jade, was currently chewing on some carrots. And then, directly above Jade, there was my grandmother sleeping in midair, which made for a very strange sight. She was floating horizontally next to my desk. Her mouth was wide open, and she was letting out some seriously earth-shattering snores. It was a good thing nonmagical humans couldn't sense overspirits at all. Otherwise we'd probably be getting noise complaints from all around the city.

"Lao Lao," I shouted. "Wake up!"

It took a few more shouts before my grandmother snorted and jolted, slowly rolling up into a sitting position. Lao Lao blinked the sleep out of her eyes and yawned, staring at me. "Oh, Winnie. Did you have a good day at school?"

"School was fine," I said impatiently. "Are we going to train now?"

"You're very eager today," my grandmother remarked, eyeing me with approval. "You were never in a hurry for shaman training before meeting with the Spirit Council."

"Well, yeah. There's a class three spirit we need to track down and catch. Plus, I need to capture fifty rogue spirits if I want to advance to level one," I explained, pointing at my Shaman Task Force badge. "I can't go around as a *rookie*. People will think I have no idea what I'm doing."

"You don't have any idea what you're doing, though."

I scowled. "Okay, but people don't need to *know* that." Plus, *rookie* just sounded bad. I definitely didn't want to hold on to that title for any longer than necessary.

"There's no need to rush to level up in the Shaman Task Force. Everyone goes at their own pace. And besides, everyone starts out as a rookie, Winnie," explained Lao Lao. A misty look came over her face. "Why, I was a rookie just like you, once. Though I was a little younger when I got my badge—nine years old, if I recall."

Of course. Anything I could do, my prodigious grandmother had done earlier, not to mention better. "How long did it take you to advance to level one?" I almost didn't want to know the answer.

"Hmm . . ." Lao Lao stroked her chin and squinted at a crack in the ceiling. "Two days, I think?"

"WHAT?"

"Yes, but don't worry, Winnie—times were different back then. Very, very different. There was none of this new-fangled technology." Lao Lao waved her hand at my phone, giving it a mistrusting look. "My hometown was overrun with rogue spirits during those days. Could hardly turn the corner without bumping into one or two. It was very easy capturing fifty spirits to reach level one status. Why, I did it and still had time to go to school and have three square meals!" She chuckled.

Great. Lao Lao had only taken two days to capture fifty spirits and reach level one. No wonder the Spirit Council had praised her so much. Since I was related to her, the Spirit Council members probably expected to see a similar level of mastery from me. I wanted more than anything to show them what I was capable of, especially that Zhula.

Given what the Spirit Council had told me, Halloween—and the lead-up to that day—should have been the ideal time to capture plenty of rogue spirits and level up. So far, though, I hadn't sensed any spirits lingering about. The evilest presence in Groton right now was Lisa after getting a bad test score. My sister could be *scary* when she was in a foul mood.

"David's downstairs," I said abruptly, changing the subject before Lao Lao could casually mention more superhuman feats she'd achieved when she was younger than me. "I told him we could train together today."

"Ah, David! How wonderful." My grandmother's face lit up. Then, just as quickly, it drooped, as though an unpleasant thought had occurred to her. "Oh . . . does that mean Joe is here, too?"

"Joe is here, too," I confirmed.

"Tell them I'm sick." My grandmother turned over in midair, facing away from me.

"I can't do that! You're a spirit. Spirits don't get sick."

"We spirits absolutely do get sick," Lao Lao retorted. "For example, right now, I am very sick of that turd *Joe* standing in our house."

"That's . . . not the kind of *sick* I meant, Lao Lao." For an old lady, my grandmother could be very childish sometimes. She and Joe had a rivalry that stretched back to their shaman days. Even now they weren't over it, and I was certain that if it weren't for David and me, they'd spend all their free time going at each other. Honestly, adults can be such kids.

"Fine. Tell them I'm dead, then," said my grandmother.

"You . . . are dead."

"Tell them I died again."

It was useless trying to persuade Lao Lao when she got like this. Sighing, I turned around, only to realize that the doorway was blocked—by David and his pet iguana, Qianlong, who was sitting on David's left shoulder. Qianlong was no ordinary iguana—at least not anymore. Just like how Lao Lao was anchored to Jade, David's overspirit, Joe, was anchored to Qianlong. At the moment, it seemed like Joe's spirit was inside Qianlong, because Joe was nowhere in sight.

I wondered if Qianlong and Jade ever got uncomfortable with overspirits inside them, or if they even noticed.

"You were taking forever, so I came up here," explained

David. He glanced over at Lao Lao, who was pointedly looking away from Qianlong. "Ā yí?" he said politely.

"Oh, David." My grandmother beamed at him. David had that sort of Goody Two-shoes charm that made all the Asian aunties croon over him, as though he could do no wrong. It was unfair. "How are you?"

Before David could reply, Qianlong scurried from David's left shoulder to his right. The iguana fixed its great black eyes on me in a way that made me feel like it was peering into my soul.

Then, after a moment, a silvery spirit emerged out of Qianlong, turning into the now-familiar form of David's relative. Joe's emperor robes billowed about him, and he reached up to brush off his fancy hat. "Napping all day, were you, Yipei?" Joe sneered at my grandmother. "I meditated at dawn, and then spent my day elevating my mind with great literature and impressionistic artwork."

Lao Lao raised an eyebrow. "What literature? What artwork?"

In response, Joe lifted his nose high into the air. "Never you mind. It's all above your caliber, I'm afraid."

"He came across my old picture books," David whispered to me. "He really likes *The Very Hungry Caterpillar.*"

I sensed it was time to interrupt before the two spirits were at each other's throats. The last thing we needed was to waste time breaking up a fight between Lao Lao and Joe.

"David and I need to capture fifty spirits apiece in order

to become level one agents," I said, putting my hands on my hips. I wondered if this was what Mama and Baba felt like when they had to scold Lisa and me for misbehaving. "The Spirit Council also gave us a mission to track down a rogue class three spirit. We have a lot of work ahead of us, so the both of you have to set aside your differences and help us out. Okay?"

Lao Lao and Joe were glaring at each other so intensely, I swear electricity crackled in the air between them.

Though at first I'd found Joe's and Lao Lao's competitive relationship to be a bit amusing, now it was just frustrating. Of course, they had already died and become spirits, so they didn't have to prove anything to anyone. But their bickering was wasting *my* precious time. How were David and I ever going level up and prove ourselves as shamans if our overspirits couldn't even look at each other without blurting out insults?

Joe and Lao Lao harrumphed and glared in opposite directions.

"Don't be immature, Yipei. The children have an important mission," Joe chastised.

"Me? You were the one who started being rude to me. I was just minding my own business," Lao Lao said.

David shot me an exasperated look. I gave a helpless shrug.

But then, miraculously, Joe was the first to cave. "In the name of the mission, I'm willing to put up with you for now." That was probably the nicest thing he'd ever said to Lao Lao.

My grandmother rolled her eyes. I could tell it was taking every last ounce of her patience not to snap at Joe. "Fine. As long as you're nice, I'll be nice."

"You children are going to that Museum of Thingy tomorrow, aren't you?" Joe asked.

"Um, if you mean the Museum of Art History, then yeah," I said. "Why?"

The old man stroked his silvery beard, a thoughtful look in his eyes. "There's a Chinese art exhibit there," he explained. "It's possible that there *may* be enough history there to potentially draw an otherworldly being . . . say, a class three spirit."

"Ah." Lao Lao nodded. "That is a possibility."

"You're suggesting that the class three spirit might be at the *museum?*" David said in disbelief.

"Why would they go through all the trouble of breaking out of the spirit realm just to hang around a boring old museum?" I blurted out. If I were a chaotic spirit and went through all that effort to escape into the human world, I'd go somewhere cool, like Disney World. Just saying.

"It's just a theory," Joe said defensively. He scowled. "I don't see you two coming up with any other leads."

David and I exchanged a look, and I bit my lip. Joe was right. As we didn't have any other clues to go off of, we might as well check out the exhibit during the field trip.

"Also, those museum curators have my old calligraphy set," Joe added. He pointed at David. "You'll get it back for me, of course."

"I can't do that!" David's face drained of color, as though the overspirit had asked him to commit a crime . . . which I guess he had. "That's stealing! It's illegal."

"It's not stealing if the museum swiped the calligraphy set from me in the first place," Joe sniffed. "And someone stole my favorite pair of fuzzy slippers, too. I knew I should've buried all my precious treasures with me when I died."

"I don't think your fuzzy slippers are on display at the Museum of Art History," I said.

"Winnie and David, don't steal anything from the museum, please." My grandmother threw Joe a pointed look, and he stuck his tongue out at her. "But when you're at the museum tomorrow, keep your eyes peeled for any sign of spirit activity, or anything that could serve as a hint. Better yet, take Joe and me with you."

"No," David and I said at once, causing our overspirits to frown at us. Even though Lao Lao and Joe kept insisting on following us around, their presence would draw attention to us even though they were invisible. Those overspirits never kept their mouths shut, forcing us to reply to what would appear to be thin air.

Now David and I really had to capture that class three spirit. And though part of me hoped we'd discover a worthwhile lead at the Museum of Art History, another part of me was hoping that Joe was wrong. Because if he *was* right, he was never going to shut up about it. The only thing more insufferable than Joe was Joe with bragging rights for all eternity.

CHAPTER FOUR

The next day was the sixth-grade class trip to the Museum of Art History.

"For the last time, I can't take you into the museum," I told my grandmother when she insisted, yet again, that she tag along. "I'm sorry." Though I was pretending to be crushed about it, I was pretty elated. Lao Lao had taken to hovering around me everywhere all the time. I'd signed up to be an agent for the Shaman Task Force, not a round-the-clock babysitter for the spirit of my grandmother. I didn't get paid enough for that. I didn't get paid at all.

"Why not?" Lao Lao whined, pouting and crossing her arms over her chest.

I didn't miss the irony of me having to tell my grandmother to behave, instead of the other way around. "Since you can't travel separately from Jade, I'd have to bring her, too. Rabbits *definitely* aren't allowed in museums. The security guards are going to check our bags."

Because Lao Lao had crossed over from the spirit realm through Jade, she was still anchored to the rabbit and couldn't travel very far from Jade. During the Mid-Autumn

Festival, Lao Lao's presence here in the human world had grown strong enough that she could sometimes separate from Jade, but that power had faded after the holiday ended. I wasn't complaining, though. This was probably a good thing for my social life, or else my grandmother would follow me around outside the house as well, upending everything.

Lao Lao frowned, worry lines creasing her brow. "But what if something happens while you're there? What if that class three spirit attacks? I can't be there to protect you."

"I'll force the spirit to sit there and listen to the tour guide. It'll die of boredom, I guarantee it."

"Winnie, this is no time for your jokes!"

If you ask me, my humor never gets the appreciation it deserves around here. "Fine. But seriously, I'll be okay. Baba is coming along to chaperone the field trip."

Lao Lao's eyebrows raised. "Really? Oh, that's good. Even if he doesn't have an ounce of magic in his blood."

It *was* good. I planned to make the most of Baba being there for my field trip.

"It would be even better if I accompanied you, too, Winnie," my grandmother said pointedly.

Lao Lao was going to keep pressing me until the moment I was out of earshot, probably. "Nothing will happen. Museums are boring as heck. Plus, David will be there with me, remember? I'm sure even if there's an emergency, our combined powers would keep a spirit at bay." Even though I forced myself to sound confident, the thought of the rogue class three spirit still rang in the back of my head. All I wanted to do was enjoy the field trip—and get to spend time with Baba—but I couldn't. My gut told me that danger lurked around the corner, even though everything in Groton had been peaceful since the Mid-Autumn Festival. Was this going to be life from now on, since I'd dedicated myself to being part of the Shaman Task Force?

Lao Lao was giving me a worried look, so I tried to smile reassuringly. "I'll be back before you know it, Lao Lao."

My grandmother finally relented, sensing that I wouldn't change my mind. So I headed down the stairs, with a slight spring in my step.

As soon as I entered the kitchen, I found Lisa putting her empty cereal bowl into the sink, rushing around and looking frazzled. It seemed she was late for school again.

"Where's Baba?" I asked, glancing around the kitchen. "He's supposed to take me to school and chaperone my field trip today."

Lisa paused, staring at me in confusion. "Baba? He already left for work. I heard the car leave, like, twenty minutes ago."

My stomach dropped. "What? Are you sure?" That couldn't be right. Had my father decided to head to my school before me? But why would he do that?

My sister scrunched her face at me. "Duh. Why would I make that up?" Shaking her head, she hurried past me without another word.

I stood there, feeling silly. Then a stomach-sinking thought struck me. Had my father just completely forgotten about his promise to me?

Quickly, I texted Baba.

> **Winnie:** Are you still chaperoning my class field trip today?

> **Baba:** That's today?

> **Winnie:** Yeah . . .

> **Baba:** I had to come in to work. Sorry I forgot. Busy morning. I will email your teacher

For a moment, I didn't even know what to feel. Then the disappointment hit me like a punch to the gut. I sat down on the chair, feeling defeated. I should have expected this. I should have never gotten my hopes up.

It had always gone like this. Back in elementary school, I used to invite my parents to field trips and choir performances, and Mama was the only one who would come. For once, I'd let myself hope that Baba would show up to a school event. And that had been a big mistake. I should've expected that my father would forget about chaperoning my field trip. Work always came first for him.

"I wish I had a father who had time for me," I said to no

one in particular, my frustration getting the better of me. In the empty kitchen, the lights seemed to dim for just a moment, as though someone were listening to me. But that was just wishful thinking.

Blinking back tears, I shook my head and grabbed a cereal bar out of the pantry. There was no time to mope around. I needed to get to school.

Even though I'm not the biggest fan of museums—you try looking at statues and artifacts for hours and hours on end without falling asleep—I was still looking forward to this trip. No matter the destination, school field trips were always fun. You'd be away from school for all or most of the day, which meant teachers couldn't spring quizzes on you or anything horrible like that. Sometimes, if you were lucky, the teachers and parents would buy you lunch or yummy treats.

The Museum of Art History is a fairly popular museum located in downtown Groton. It's one of two things our town is known for. The second thing is for having a water tower that also happens to be the world's largest mustard bottle. In the summer, Groton even hosts an annual mustard festival. No town in America loves mustard more than Groton.

Anyway, after morning announcements, the sixth graders got to leave school during first period for the all-day trip to the Museum of Art History. The two sixth-grade homerooms crammed together onto two yellow school buses and made the half-hour drive to the museum. The chaperoning parents drove separately.

As I passed Mrs. Payton on my way to the bus, I quickly mumbled, "Sorry my dad couldn't make it." It wasn't like it was my fault, but I still felt embarrassed. After all, my teacher had expected Baba to show up today, and I'd even told a few other classmates about it, too . . . and then Baba had gone and flaked.

"Ah, no worries, Winnie," said Mrs. Payton brightly. "We had more than enough parents sign up to volunteer." She didn't seem to mind that Baba couldn't make it any longer, which was good. The last thing I wanted was for Baba's absence to stress out my teacher.

I sat next to David on the bus. Well, I *tried* to sit alone, setting my Pusheen backpack in the space next to me so there was no room for anyone to sit. That was a clear signal for everyone to stay out of my personal bubble.

"Two students per seat," said David's teacher, Mr. Burnside, who was sitting in the seat one row up and over from me. "We won't start the bus until every student is seated, and there will be *two* students per seat." Mr. Burnside glared at me, which made it pretty clear who he was talking to. Oops. I finally picked up my backpack to let David scoot in.

"Man, I've been excited about this field trip forever," David said, unzipping his backpack and elbowing me in the process.

This was exactly why I wanted to sit alone. Annoyed, I rubbed the spot where David had elbowed me. "Yeah, I know." He'd only told me, like, ten times already.

"I didn't finish telling you about the museum yesterday. It's got art-history exhibits for thirty-seven different countries. I'm most looking forward to seeing the Chinese art exhibit," said David eagerly. David had this habit of talking at lightning speed when he was excited. I could barely follow what he was saying. "Remember that calligraphy set Joe mentioned yesterday? It's a precious family heirloom. He lost it five centuries ago. Or, rather, he said that the colonizers stole it. His words, not mine. Apparently Joe's mother got really mad at him for that." He took a deep breath. It was so loud that it made me feel out of breath just hearing it. "Anyway, why are you excited to visit the museum?"

"Uh . . . I wanted to get out of class," I admitted.

David frowned at me. I shrugged. Hey, I was just saying what the rest of us were thinking. Even though I'm a pretty good student and like learning, it's nice to have a day off every once in a while.

Without Baba there, now I was just trying to enjoy the fact that I didn't have to go to my classes today. Especially gym class. Any day where I didn't have to breathe smelly locker-room air was an excellent day in my books.

Lowering his voice so that nobody else could hear him, David whispered, "Hopefully nothing, you know, *abnormal* happens." His eyes flickered around the bus, as though he thought we might get ambushed by evil spirits right here and now.

"Of course nothing's going to happen," I said, trying to sound completely confident. We didn't exactly have reason to suspect that something *would* happen today. "Nothing has happened so far, right? And in seven hours we'll be reunited with our overspirits again."

"Right," David said, though he was biting his lip.

David's nervousness was making *me* tense. It was time to change the subject. "So you were saying about thirty-seven exhibits . . . ?" I prompted.

That was all David needed to launch into a detailed explanation of each exhibit, completely turning his mood around. David was pretty easy to handle now that I had him all figured out.

The ride over went by fast. Nothing more eventful happened than my homeroom teacher, Mrs. Payton, spilling her coffee all over Mr. Burnside's dress shirt when the bus took a sharp turn. That was funny, except not so much for Mrs. Payton, who was at the receiving end of Mr. Burnside's death glare. Mr. Burnside could teach a class on glaring.

When we pulled into the museum parking lot, the teachers ordered us to form a single-file line to get off the bus in an orderly fashion. I stared up at the tall white building. Outside, there was a sign that read MUSEUM OF ART HISTORY.

The air-conditioning hit me full blast as we entered the building. A guide was already waiting for us, an older lady with a badge on her uniform that said HI, MY NAME IS MILDRED KANE. Mildred sounded exactly like the name of somebody who would work at a museum.

Mildred welcomed us and began taking us around the museum. We first stopped by the Roman art exhibit. There were marble statues of gods, goddesses, and random old philosophers for some reason. There were also pretty paintings that Mildred called "abstract"; they looked like a bunch of colorful splotches to me. In fact, I was pretty sure I had been creating at that level in my kindergarten finger-painting classes.

A kid from Mr. Burnside's class, Spencer, raised his hand.

"Yes?" said Mildred.

"Mrs. Kane, why is this considered art when it looks like a bunch of scribbles?" Spencer asked loudly.

Mildred's face turned red as a few students broke out into giggles. Spencer looked around with a grin on his face, his chest puffed out. Well, he was pretty much just saying what was on everyone's mind.

Mr. Burnside quickly intercepted. "That's enough, Spencer. No silly questions are allowed. Mildred, please proceed with the tour."

"Oh, a-all right," said Mildred, shaking her head. "If you'll follow me, students . . ."

"Hey, wanna go check out the Chinese exhibit now?" David whispered to me as Mildred led us into the Egyptian room next.

I blinked at him. "You're suggesting we *ditch our group?*" That was probably the least David-like suggestion ever. The David I knew would sooner eat worms than ditch class.

"Shhhh! Not so loud. Our group is only getting farther from the Chinese art exhibit, so if we wanna check it out, we have to ditch." David glanced around with a nervous look, as though expecting Mrs. Payton to come swooping down on us at any moment.

But nobody was paying attention to us. About half the students were listening to Mildred, while the other half were huddled and talking among themselves. Jessamyn, Tracy, and Kim had begun braiding each other's hair. Mr. Burnside and Mrs. Payton were locked in some kind of glaring contest, clearly still fighting over the coffee spill earlier. They were oblivious to whatever was happening around them. If David and I *did* try to slip away from the group, now was the moment.

"Okay, let's go." Even though I wasn't sensing any spirit activity and *seriously* doubted we'd find any useful information, it couldn't hurt to take a look. "Do you even know where the Chinese exhibit is?"

David stared at me like I'd asked him if the sky was blue. "Of course. As I've said, I've been here before. Going to museums is a bit of a hobby of mine. Some of us like to stimulate our minds in our free time, Winnie." He turned up his nose.

I rolled my eyes. David *would* spend his free time

browsing museums. Just like he probably memorized the thesaurus for fun.

He pointed toward a hall behind us. "Anyway, the Chinese exhibit is right down there. We'll just go there and be back before anyone even notices we're gone. If anyone says anything, we'll claim we were lost."

"Okay."

With David leading, we edged away from our group. Mildred was walking everyone deeper into the Egyptian art room. Nobody was paying us any attention at all as we put more distance between us and our classes. Then they disappeared into the room, and David and I were speeding in the opposite direction.

The Chinese exhibit was practically empty when we entered. There were only two other people that I could see inside: an old man and an old woman. It made sense that the place would be empty midmorning on a Wednesday. Everyone else would be at school or work.

I swept my gaze from wall to wall, holding my breath, ready to fight the *instant* a spirit leapt at me. But of course there was nothing out of the ordinary here. I was relieved, mostly, but also a tiny bit disappointed. Another potential lead—gone.

"Whoa," I said as I glanced around the room. There were displays of ancient artwork in glass cases in the middle of the room, as well as tall cases that lined the walls. The displays contained everything from colorful traditional clothing to calligraphy. There were signs in front of each piece of artwork explaining what it was, as well as which dynasty it was from.

"Joe claims that a lot of these artifacts were stolen from China, not freely given," David explained with a sour look on his face.

"Really? How are they allowed to hang in museums, then?"

He shrugged. "'History is written by the victors.' Ever heard that quote? I've been reading up on Chinese art history, and it turns out . . ."

I stopped to admire a scroll from the Ming dynasty, while David wandered farther into the room, pretty much talking to himself. If what David said was true, then had this scroll been stolen, too? Mama and Baba had drilled into Lisa and me that we should never take anything that didn't belong to us. You'd think adults would know better, but I guess not.

Out of the corner of my eye, I spotted movement behind one of the glass cases, which contained a long golden robe. I heard something, too. Voices whispered in what sounded like Mandarin, but I couldn't hear the words.

Curious, I walked over, and the voices grew louder. At the same time, the noise level of the world around me grew quieter. The sound of my class's tour group became distant and muffled, and then I couldn't hear them at all.

A faint fragrance wafted into my nostrils—the scent of flowers. But where was it coming from? There didn't seem to be anyone nearby. The perfume wasn't flowery,

anyway—rather, it smelled like fresh flowers and spring-
time.

Now, a bit closer to the glass case, I could make out what
the voices were saying.

"... summoned ... have power ... stolen ... *soon* ..."

What I saw nearly caused me to stumble into the nearest
display. Right before my eyes, the long golden robe vanished into thin air.

"Ack!" I shouted in surprise.

That wasn't even the end of it. Some black mass was
swirling on the wall behind the case, growing larger and
larger, until it was at least three feet in width and length. A
portal. As I watched in disbelief, it swirled around, giving
the appearance of a long, winding tunnel that seemed to
lead farther and farther into darkness.

I should have been frightened. I should have known that
it was time to get out of the Chinese art exhibit. And on
some level, I did register both thoughts. Still, my curiosity
outweighed my fear, and I touched the glass case.

Then something *whoosh*ed out of the portal.

CHAPTER FIVE

My first, frantic thought was that it had been a really, *really* bad idea to leave my overspirit at home today.

"AGHHHHHH!" I screamed.

"What's wrong?" David came running over at the sound of my scream. Weird. Only David's voice hadn't grown quiet with the rest of the world.

"I heard v-voices—and then s-something came out of there—" I stumbled back, pointing at the place where there had been a black portal seconds ago. But now it had vanished. There was nothing behind the glass display. I blinked once, twice, three times, to make sure my eyes weren't playing tricks on me, but no. There was no portal, no anything. Just a plain, bare, boring wall.

In a beat, the noise level of the world returned to me, so disorienting that I had to shake my head as the loud chatter of museum visitors returned. It was as though the world around me had frozen for a long moment when that portal appeared—and when it vanished, time and everything else came rushing back.

Now, instead of feeling fear or curiosity, I was utterly

confused. What had happened just now? Could I have imagined the portal, the voices, and that flowery fragrance?

David gave me a funny look. "You heard . . . voices? What?"

"I . . . I swear there was something there a moment ago," I said, though my certainty was weakening. It was hard to be sure of what I'd seen, especially with David staring at me like I'd sprouted a third hand.

"What kind of something?" David's eyes widened in realization and horror, and he spun around with his arms up, like he expected to be tackled to the floor. "Wait—like, spirits?"

"Maybe? I'm not sure. I saw something . . . um . . ." Now feeling a bit stupid, I struggled to formulate an answer. "I think I saw . . . a portal? And I think it's the portal that the class three spirit has been using!"

"So you *did* see a spirit," David yelped. He already had a hand raised to his Shaman Task Force badge, as though he was about to speed-dial the Spirit Council.

"Wait—I didn't *see* any spirits," I clarified. The last thing I wanted was for us to act rashly and call the Spirit Council for no reason. Or, even worse, to call them because I had an overactive imagination. That would make me look *really* great. "I just heard . . . them. Or at least I heard voices."

"Voices," David repeated. "Plural? As in multiple spirits?"

"I think so? Oh! And I smelled them, too. I think. Flowers?"

"You think these spirits smell like . . . flowers?" I could

tell David was getting annoyed with me, like he thought I'd made a big deal out of nothing. His eyebrows were rising further and further. If they got any higher, they'd disappear into his hairline.

The worst part was that I couldn't blame him. Evil spirits that smelled like flowers? Who would believe something as silly as that? Evil spirits should smell like dirty underwear or something. That was how they always smelled in stories.

"Are you sure you didn't just hear the voices of other people in the museum?" David asked. "If there were spirits here, wouldn't we have sensed them by now? Like, we'd probably feel chills or something." He rubbed his shoulders, demonstrating.

That was a good point. During the Mid-Autumn Festival, David and I had been able to sense the presence of evil spirits. They had been accompanied by a chill that had ended up freezing many residents of Groton. This time, I hadn't felt a chill. I hadn't felt the temperature change at all.

Now that David mentioned it, how could I be certain that what I'd heard wasn't merely the voices of the old man and old woman in the room? They were on the far side of the exhibit, but maybe their voices had traveled over to us. This exhibit was pretty quiet, after all. And that black portal I'd seen, or thought I'd seen—had it really been a portal? Maybe it had been a trick of the light. Maybe I thought I'd had a supernatural experience, because I *wanted* to believe that we had a lead on our class three spirit. The more time that passed, the less certain I was about what I'd seen and heard.

"Okay, never mind." I blushed. It was time to change the subject, even if I still didn't believe that what I'd seen, heard, and smelled had been a result of an overactive imagination. I did my best to ignore the weird lingering feeling that I couldn't quite shake. "Did you find Joe's old calligraphy set?"

David scrunched his nose. "Well, I found *a* calligraphy set. No idea if it's his. But I took a picture of it for him to look at later. Hang on—why is that glass case empty now?" He pointed to the case, eyes narrowed. "Wasn't there something in there before?"

"There was a golden robe in there before," I said.

"Well, what happened to it?" David asked, baffled.

"It . . . It vanished. When the portal appeared."

He shook his head. "That's so weird . . . maybe this *is* the doing of evil spirits."

I didn't know what was going on. I just knew I didn't want to stay here an instant longer. Who knew what other strange things might happen? Besides, if something evil was lurking about, then there was a huge group of people—our teachers and classmates—currently strolling around for them to attack. And with or without my overspirit, it was still my duty as a member of the Shaman Task Force to protect the people of Groton from supernatural harm.

"Let's get back to our group," I suggested. "Just in case there *are* spirits around."

"Yeah, good idea. Plus, they might notice our absence soon. We've been gone for a while," David pointed out.

Together, we sped out of the Chinese art exhibit back toward the Egyptian one, trying to put as much space as possible between us and the disappearing black hole.

We hurried past the displays of mummies and cool-looking vases. I spotted a couple of familiar-looking kids from David's homeroom hanging toward the back of the group. They looked up when David and I casually rejoined. Quickly, I pretended to be engrossed in examining a small mummy statue.

"Hey, where'd you two go?" the one closest to us— I think his name was Trevor—asked.

"We've been here all along," I said.

"No, you haven't," Trevor replied stubbornly. I glared at him, sending him a silent message to let this go, but he stood his ground.

"Hey, Trevor, your shoelaces are untied," David said, pointing down at the floor.

Trevor glanced down. "Huh? No, they aren't."

David grabbed my hand, and we disappeared into the group, closer to where Mr. Burnside and Mrs. Payton were. The teachers didn't seem to notice that we'd been gone, and nobody else questioned us. Success. Even more important, there was no sign of any strange, otherworldly activity around the group.

Still, I couldn't quite shake off the lingering sensation that something *had* shifted in the air. That today, at the museum, I'd witnessed something that I shouldn't have.

And I had a feeling that David's and my jobs as rookie agents were about to get a whole lot tougher.

CHAPTER SIX

"You good, Winnie? You've been acting weird ever since we left the museum. Well, actually you've been weird since the day I met you, but you know, you're being weirder than usual today."

I rolled my eyes, resisting the urge to run into David's bike with mine. We were pedaling back home from school. Our class had stayed at the museum for a couple more hours after that strange incident at the Chinese art exhibit. Nothing else eventful happened during the field trip, unless you counted Mr. Burnside getting his revenge on Mrs. Payton's coffee spill by "accidentally" dripping the mayo from his sandwich onto her hand. The pterodactyl-like screech Mrs. Payton let out was probably heard all around the world.

Still, I hadn't been able to shake an unsettled feeling since departing from that exhibit. I really didn't think I'd imagined the golden robe disappearing, nor the black portal that had mysteriously appeared and then vanished.

If I'd had to guess, something had happened in the spirit realm when I went back there—perhaps I'd disturbed that rogue class three spirit, or perhaps more spirits had escaped into our world. That would mean David and I needed to capture them before they began causing chaos in Groton. First I needed to get back to my grandmother as soon as I could. Lao Lao would know what was going on, and what to do about it. She always did.

"Slow down your pedaling, will you? Are you training for the Olympics?" David yelled over the wind.

In response, I pedaled even faster. "I've got something important to do. I'll see you later!" I didn't wait to hear David's response before rounding the corner, making a bee-line straight for my house.

When I got home, I bounded up the stairs. Lisa was home, judging by the Taylor Swift song loudly blasting from her room. Hopefully she wouldn't be able to hear me over the music.

"Lao Lao, I need your help!" I whisper-yelled. My grand-mother was already awake when I entered my room. Awake and alert, with her arms crossed over her chest and an impatient expression on her face, as though she'd been counting down the moments until I got back from school. Come to think of it, she probably had.

Jade was running around in rapid circles in her cage, which was abnormal. My pet rabbit only had two modes: eating or sleeping (a rabbit after my own heart). It seemed that perhaps I wasn't the only one who'd sensed that something was off in Groton.

"There are spirits on the loose, Winnie," my grand-mother said. She pressed her fingers to her temples, and then she closed her eyes. "I'm glad you came back quickly. I didn't sense them before you left, but that changed about an hour ago."

"I knew something was wrong," I blurted. "That stupid David. He made me feel like I was the silly one for thinking that there were spirits around." I paused. "Wait, but I don't feel a chill this time."

"That chill was due specifically to the Gloomy One's—Hou Yi's—influence," Lao Lao said. "The most powerful spirits will have their own unique impact on the human world. Though it's true that it seems these new spirits are much harder to detect than the others. . . ." As she spoke, her forehead creased, as though it was taking all her concentration to sense these spirits.

I remembered how I'd detected that flowery smell at the museum. "Oh. I *do* think I sensed something earlier."

Lao Lao opened her eyes and narrowed them at me. "Did something happen while you were away on the field trip?"

"Um . . . yes, but I'm not sure exactly what happened. We went to the museum, and there was this one exhibit—it had Chinese artifacts and history. I walked toward the back, and I thought I saw . . . something weird. A golden robe vanished into thin air. And there was this black portal."

"A portal?" Alarm caused my grandmother's voice to get sharper. "Between the human and spirit worlds? No, this isn't good, not good at all." She muttered something to herself, under her breath, but I couldn't hear her.

"The portal's closed now, though," I offered weakly. "Oh, and—and I also heard strange voices and smelled something flowery."

Lao Lao's expression went from concerned to confused. "Flowers? I can't recall any evil spirits that smell like flowers. What did the voices say?"

I struggled to remember. "I couldn't hear much. They said something about . . . summoning?"

"Well, that's certainly unusual. But just in case, given the fast approach of Halloween, we should prepare more thoroughly for any potential spirit attacks."

A panicked thought struck me. "Sure, but . . . I'm out of mooncakes!" During the Mid-Autumn Festival, I'd unlocked the full extent of my powers by baking and eating magical mooncakes from Lao Lao's recipe book. That was how I'd been able to take down the powerful spirit of Hou Yi.

"You don't need mooncakes," Lao Lao said. "They won't help us in this situation."

"They won't?"

"Because it was the Mid-Autumn Festival, and you were specifically facing the spirit of Hou Yi, the mooncakes were the most effective weapon against him and his minions. They won't be as effective now that the Mid-Autumn Festival has passed."

"So—so what *am* I supposed to use, then?" Last I'd checked, the pages of Lao Lao's recipe book had been glued together, making it impossible for me to access any magical recipes besides the one for the mooncake. If I couldn't really use those anymore, then I'd lost the most effective weapon in my arsenal.

"You'll know soon enough," my grandmother answered mysteriously. "The next recipe will unlock for you once the need arises. For the moment, you and I must—"

My grandmother's words were interrupted by the sound of an insistent knock on my bedroom door. Too late, I realized Lisa's music had turned off.

"Winnie? Hello? I know you're in there—I heard you talking!"

Leave it to Lisa to interrupt me when I was in the middle of something important. Resigning myself, I headed over to the door and opened it. My sister had tied her hair back in a tight bun. She was wearing a pink oversized hoodie paired with pink sweatpants, which I recognized as her studying outfit. She was also wearing a frown, which I recognized as her default expression.

"Were you talking to yourself in there?" Lisa said, craning her neck to see over my shoulder. Of course, my sister didn't have shaman powers and couldn't see the spirit of our grandmother hovering in the background. "You're so weird, Winnie."

"What do you want?" I huffed. If Lisa had come into my room just to bug me, she'd chosen the wrong day.

"Mama asked me to pick up a few things from Super 196," Lisa explained. Super 196 is the local Asian supermarket, where my family gets the majority of our groceries. I'm pretty sure Super 196 owes at least 50 percent of their profit to us alone. "You're coming with me."

"What? Why? I don't have time to go grocery shopping. I . . . I have . . . uh . . . I have homework," I blurted out, which was perfectly true. I had a lot of homework. And I had a lot of shaman work, too, but Lisa didn't need to know about that part.

"Well, I have more homework than you," Lisa said, rolling her eyes. "Two of us can get the job done faster than one."

"But—"

"Great. Meet me outside the house in five." Without waiting for a response from me, Lisa whirled around and headed back to her room.

I sighed. Even peacekeeping shamans still had to do mundane tasks like grocery shopping sometimes.

It took Lisa and me about ten minutes to bike over to Super 196. As we biked, I realized it had been a while since my sister and I had hung out together—even only to get groceries. Lisa had been getting busier and busier these days. Though I'd thought maybe we'd be closer after I'd saved her during the Mid-Autumn Festival, things hadn't panned out that way at all.

"By the way, why'd you bring your backpack with you?" Lisa asked, glancing over at me.

"Um . . . habit." I blurted out the first explanation I could think of. It wasn't like I could tell my sister the truth. *I'm carrying my pet rabbit and the spirit of our grandmother in my backpack, in case I have to fight any evil spirits at Super 196.* Yeah, that would go over well.

"You refused to bring me along to the Museum of Art History, and look what happened there," Lao Lao had said when I'd first insisted on going without her. "No, I'm not letting you out of my sight, Winnie."

I seriously didn't think a trip to the grocery store could get violent, but better safe than sorry. So I'd put Jade in my backpack, only zipping it about three-quarters of the way so that she could breathe in there. I'd grabbed a mason jar and stuffed it into the backpack, too, just in case we ran into any rogue spirits.

Once we arrived at Super 196, Lisa and I locked our bikes on the rack outside the grocery store, grabbed a shopping cart, and headed inside. Immediately, we were greeted with the sharp, distinct smell of Asian grocery stores—like so many different spices mixing together. There were aisles that carried every kind of spice you could imagine, as well as produce, rice, and even fish.

My eyes landed immediately on the snack aisles, which were filled with every delicious treat from Choco Pies to White Rabbit candy to dried plums to hawthorn flakes.

Lao Lao tsked. "Those sweets will rot your teeth."

"I knew I should've left you at home," I muttered under my breath.

"Winnie, over here!" Lisa waved me over from the spice aisle.

I started to head over, but then stopped in my tracks. Someone had come up behind Lisa and started chatting with her. By the lanky profile and spiky black hair, I could tell it was David's older brother, Luke. David was nowhere in sight, though.

I snickered. Luke had always had an obvious thing for Lisa. Now my sister was single, so maybe something would actually happen between them. It was better for me to stay out of their way. I was too far to hear what they were saying, so I slowly crept forward—and then was startled by a loud crash behind me. It sounded like something expensive had broken.

I whirled around and saw that a large, flower-covered vase had tipped over. A disgruntled-looking employee had already begun to sweep up the pieces, while customers stepped away from the mess.

"Hold on, Winnie. I sense . . . something here. It may be a spirit, drawn to you, a shaman."

I glanced over at Lao Lao, whose expression had turned tense. My heart leapt. There was a good chance that that crash had come from a supernatural force—a spirit. And not a small one, either.

My fingers flew to the Shaman Task Force badge on my shirt, and I was about to call for help, but then I hesitated.

No, I couldn't go running to the Spirit Council for every little thing. First I wanted to try to handle this emergency on my own. This was my job, after all.

I grabbed the mason jar out of my backpack, then turned around to face the rogue spirit.

CHAPTER SEVEN

Turned out the big, bad culprit that had smashed the vase was—

"A cat?" Lao Lao and I shouted at the same time.

On the floor, in the middle of the shards of the glass vase, was a tiny gray cat, little more than the size of my hand, playing with the broken pieces. This cat was no ordinary cat, though. It was silvery and transparent, not quite here nor there, which could mean only one thing. A cat spirit. Now I was *extra* glad I hadn't called the Spirit Council right away. Zhula would laugh herself silly if I'd called them for help getting rid of a *cat*.

So much for my theory that the ruckus had been caused by a giant dangerous spirit. Though it only made sense that I'd assume such a thing. The last time a spirit had broken into our house, it had taken on the form of Lisa's exboyfriend. That spirit had completely fooled Lisa. Worse, it hadn't been anything cute, like a cat—it had been a huge, threatening bearlike spirit. Lao Lao and I had to tag-team to bring it down, even though my grandmother's spirit had only just come into the human world. Talk about learning on the fly.

But before I could feel any sense of relief, the cat shot down the snack aisle and knocked over bags of candy.

"Wh-what's going on?" cried the poor employee who'd been cleaning the mess. I supposed that to him, it looked like the candy was suddenly falling off the shelves on its own.

"What exactly is this spirit, Lao Lao?" I whispered as I crept closer toward it, unscrewing the mason-jar cap. A couple of nearby shoppers gave me strange looks, which I tried to ignore. But for the most part, people seemed to be ignoring us. Lisa and Luke were still wrapped up in their conversation several aisles over, off in their own little world.

"That's a māo guǐ," said Lao Lao. "A cat spirit. A level one spirit, but nevertheless capable of causing plenty of chaos."

"Yes, I can see that!" I dove over to try to catch the spirit in the mason jar. It took off like a lightning bolt in the other direction, leaping onto the opposite shelves.

Lao Lao also dove to catch the spirit, but it slipped just out of her reach. "Why, you little—this rascal is quite fast!"

Unless it was my imagination, this cat spirit was moving faster than any spirit we'd encountered so far, knocking over packages of food in its wake. As that thought entered my mind, I was reminded of the Spirit Council's warnings when I'd met with them to receive my badge. They'd told me to be on the lookout for spirits as Halloween drew closer. And they'd mentioned that the spirits would grow more powerful. I guess that meant they'd become speedier and harder to catch.

I lunged toward the cat, but once again it moved in a split second. This time, the cat spirit leapt up onto the topmost shelf. There it wagged its tail, as though taunting us.

Oh, great. How was I supposed to catch the māo guǐ when it was all the way up there?

Luckily my grandmother wasn't bound to the rules of gravity like I was, so she flew up and snatched the māo guǐ. But the cat spirit was slippery, and it wriggled out of her grasp. The māo guǐ jumped down from the shelf—and right into my waiting arms.

"Ha! Gotcha!" I exclaimed triumphantly. The cat spirit squirmed and nearly broke loose, but I managed to keep my grip on it somehow. With my free hand, I brought up the mason jar.

The spirit let out a wail as it was sucked into the jar. I popped on the lid, making sure it was sealed tight.

"There," I said, sighing in relief. I wiped the sweat that had formed on my brow. I shoved the spirit into my backpack. "That's one spirit down. Only forty-nine more to go before I reach level one."

Though I'd attracted a few confused looks from shoppers, they seemed to chalk up this whole scene as the antics of a kid with an overactive imagination, and nobody questioned me. *Phew.*

I looked around Super 196, assessing the damage. Aside from the broken glass and candy bags on the floor, there was nothing out of place. (In fact, Lao Lao and I were the most out-of-place objects in the grocery store.)

"You've done well, Winnie." My grandmother smiled in approval.

At Lao Lao's praise, I glowed. My grandmother didn't give out praise often, so when she did, that meant I'd done something extra special. Either that or she'd hit her head too hard at some point.

"Now let's get this māo guǐ to the Department of Supernatural Record-Keeping," said Lao Lao. "There's not a moment to waste."

"Hey! Winnie! There you are." Lisa came barreling around the corner of the aisle and placed her hands over her hips. Her cheeks were slightly red.

"Where did Luke go?" I asked, craning my neck to see around Lisa. He was nowhere in sight.

"Oh, you saw that? He, um, he already finished shopping and went home." Her blush deepened. "A-anyway, why are you still hanging around the snack aisle? Are you going to help me shop or not?"

Of course Lisa hadn't noticed a single thing that had just transpired in Super 196. She had no idea I'd captured a rogue spirit. Luke's spiky black hair probably blocked everything from her sight. Sometimes I envied Lisa's obliviousness. It seemed very peaceful.

"Um, yeah, coming." Quickly, I headed toward Lisa, and we finished getting the groceries without any further mishaps.

Lisa went home with the groceries shortly after, while I stopped at the bookstore first.

When we got to the Suntreader, I told the owner, Mr. Stevens, that I needed to go to the eighty-eighth floor. He looked confused for a moment, but then my words registered. Like magic, his face took on that now-familiar dreamy expression, and he led me to the elevators in the back of the bookstore. I was never going to get over seeing Mr. Stevens like this, all out of sorts. Magic was weird.

On the eighty-eighth floor, I stepped out of the elevator and nearly dropped the mason jar at the sight that greeted me.

"David! What're you doing here?"

David turned around. Beside him, Joe did the same. "I'm returning this spirit to the department, duh." He raised his arm to show a mason jar with the light of a captured spirit inside it. "This is the fourth one I've caught. How many have you captured so far?"

I scowled. The answer was one, but David didn't need to know that. I didn't even know when David had found the time to capture four spirits since we'd been named rookie agents. Weren't we both on the same class field trip? Did he wake up at the crack of dawn to capture spirits before school? That was totally something David would do.

In greeting, Joe just stuck his tongue out at us. It was

really, *really* hard to believe that this guy was a former emperor.

Xiao Mao, the lady with the cat head who sat behind the computer at the front desk, took our mason jars and typed something into her desktop. Then she went to search through the bookshelves, and she pulled out two books, which she brought back to the desk. Opening the jars, Xiao Mao released the spirits back into their storybooks. Then she closed the books firmly.

"Thanks for your assistance handling these pesky spirits, agents," said Xiao Mao, with a little nod toward David and me. I stood up taller.

"Xiao Mao, you haven't heard anything about . . . other spirits on the loose, have you? A class three spirit, or perhaps even stronger ones?" Lao Lao inquired. "Winnie saw a portal open here in Groton, and I'm very concerned."

"A portal? Where?" Xiao Mao asked, narrowing her eyes.

"Um . . . y-yeah. It was at the Museum of Art History," I said, sounding not certain at all. Well, I was fairly sure that my eyes weren't just playing tricks on me, but since the portal had vanished so quickly, it was hard not to second-guess myself.

Xiao Mao pushed her glasses up the bridge of her nose, frowning. "That's really not good. I'll notify the Spirit Council of the portal's location. Though I can't say no part of me saw this coming."

"What do you mean?" Joe asked.

"Aside from the class three spirit that the council has

already tasked Winnie and David with capturing, there have been . . . other disturbances in the spirit realm as of late," she replied. "As Halloween approaches, the powers of evil grow stronger here on Earth—as well as in the spirit realm. Even more powerful than during the Mid-Autumn Festival," she continued. "Please do be on alert, agents. This town will need your protection over the next few weeks."

"Yeah, so I've heard," I sighed.

"Yes, ma'am," said David. He sprung to a salute.

Even though Xiao Mao wore an ominous expression on her face, and both Joe and Lao Lao seemed nervous, I was starting to feel a little more excited. Sure, it wasn't a good thing that evil would grow stronger as Halloween approached, but it did mean that I'd have more opportunities to capture spirits and reach level one quicker. I *really* didn't want to see David advance to level one status before I did.

But more important, I'd sworn an oath to protect Groton. And boy, did this town need a *lot* of help.

CHAPTER EIGHT

Lao Lao was equally determined that I train as much as possible. Soon we fell into a routine. Training became my favorite part of the day, and I'd find myself looking forward to it during school. Yeah, it was exhausting, but a *good* kind of exhausting. It was, I imagined, the way athletes felt when they were pushing themselves toward a goal they really wanted to achieve.

I was busy from morning until late afternoon with school and extracurriculars, but for about an hour before dinner, my grandmother and I would practice combining. I'd only managed to combine with Lao Lao once since we vanquished Hou Yi during the Mid-Autumn Festival, and that had only lasted for a few seconds. If I wanted to become a powerful agent, I needed to do a lot better than that.

I wanted to try to unlock True Sight again, like I had during the Mid-Autumn Festival, but there was no way I could achieve that if I couldn't even combine with my grandmother.

"You need to relax more, Winnie," Lao Lao kept telling me. "Both your mind *and* body."

I tried *everything*. Breathing deeply to relax myself into a state where my powers would (hopefully) emerge. Stretching my arms and legs to increase blood flow (as Lao Lao recommended). I even attempted a cartwheel, which ended up with me banging my legs painfully on my bed frame.

Zhula's words circled in my head, mocking me. She'd said that many shamans could flub their way into combining with their overspirits and wielding True Sight, and that being able to master the process was the real mark of an accomplished shaman. If that was true, then I was a *long* ways away from proving myself.

On one of these days, when I was on my latest attempt to relax my mind and body—by spinning around in circles in the living room—I overheard reports of people behaving oddly. Shirley James was on the local news channel, giving the latest updates, with her new co-anchor, Jeff.

"Tonight's news involves a few strange incidents in Groton," Shirley was saying. I listened intently as I fixed myself some instant ramen for dinner. Both my parents were working late, and Lisa was volunteering for Key Club. "Over the past few days we've received separate reports of citizens behaving bizarrely. Two days ago, a mailman was seen attempting to steal the left shoe of every person he passed on the street. Yesterday, a woman tried to blow up her inflatable pool in the middle of the intersection between Heft Road and East Twelfth Mile Road, causing a traffic jam. Later that day, a man tried to rob a bank using . . . a carrot."

Jeff, who was clearly new to the business, couldn't

maintain his professional composure. He snorted. I couldn't blame him. It *was* funny news.

Ignoring her co-anchor, Shirley continued, "While these reports aren't quite cause for alarm, we urge citizens to be aware of your surroundings and alert the authorities of anyone exhibiting odd behavior. The culprits are still at large. Whether these incidents are stunts for social media or mere coincidence remains to be seen."

"This is *Shirley* not just a coincidence," said Jeff.

Shirley gave no reaction other than her smile growing tighter. Jeff was probably going to get chewed out once the camera stopped rolling.

The rest of the news was boring, but I couldn't get the reports of strange behavior out of my head. Maybe they were harmless pranks, people taking on dares for social-media clout. Or maybe there was something more sinister behind this behavior. Maybe it was linked to the rogue class three spirit somehow. When the class three spirit Hou Yi had been on the loose, a strange cold had descended upon Groton, eventually leading to people actually being frozen.

But speculating about these reports had to go to the back of my mind—at least for now. I had to deal with the more pressing matter of trying to satisfy my grandmother with my shaman training.

Because I was still getting mental blocks whenever I tried to combine with Lao Lao, my grandmother insisted that I needed to loosen up mentally and physically.

"You're overthinking," Lao Lao said. "You need to clear your mind. Don't think about the possibility of failure."

That, of course, only made me focus even *more* on the possibility of failure.

When clearing my mind didn't work, we turned to the next potential solution: loosening up my body.

My grandmother poked me in the arm. "You're too stiff. Combining with an overspirit requires flexibility of body and mind. Now loosen up. Like so." Lao Lao began shaking and shimmying her arms and legs around.

It looked like she was doing some strange dance to music that I couldn't hear. I snorted.

"Winnie, stop laughing. This is serious business!" Lao Lao said, arms above her head as she twirled around in a circle.

Quickly, I did my best to suppress the laughter. Just like my grandmother had demonstrated, I began flailing my limbs around. I only lasted a few seconds before I started cracking up again, earning me another scolding from Lao Lao.

And so training went on that day, with little result on my end, aside from me whacking my arm into the coffee table, causing a pile of books to topple over. I couldn't explain why, but I couldn't force myself back into the mindset I'd been in when I successfully combined with Lao Lao to defeat the spirit of Hou Yi.

"Let's call it a day," Lao Lao said a few days later, after

an umpteenth failed attempt at combining. "You don't want to exhaust yourself. That'll make it even harder for you to access your powers in the future."

I started to protest that I wasn't exhausted, but then my stomach interrupted me with a loud growl. Oops.

"And it's dinnertime," my grandmother said pointedly, the corners of her mouth tilting up in a smile.

I gave a sheepish grin. I *was* famished, not to mention worn out. Training was hard work, even when I was kind of failing at it.

At dinner, it was just me, Mama, and Lisa sitting around the table. I'd scarcely seen Baba since he'd flaked on chaperoning my field trip—which I was still annoyed about. Mama had gotten off work late from teaching a class at a local college, so she hadn't cooked anything fresh for dinner. Instead we were eating leftovers: beef noodle soup. It was yummy even though it was from yesterday. Mama is the *best* cook.

"Hey, loser," Lisa greeted me as I sat down at the table.

"Get away from me," I said in return.

Lisa and I have that kind of understanding only siblings could have.

"How has school been?" Mama asked, after placing steaming hot bowls of soup in front of each of us. She set a bowl on Baba's place mat, too, even though we all knew he'd be working late at the law firm again. It was a miracle if my father got home before midnight these days.

"School is okay, I guess." I shrugged and dug into my soup, slurping the noodles. The broth was perfectly savory, and the beef was just the right amount of chewy. I was in heaven.

"Your grades are still good, right?" Mama pressed.

"All A's so far," I said proudly.

Mama nodded in approval. "What about you, Lisa?"

"Um . . . about that . . . ," my sister mumbled, and then shoved a bunch of noodles into her mouth at once. She looked like a chipmunk with all that food stored in her cheeks. It was obviously a ruse to keep from having to answer Mama's question. Lisa is popular and talented at sports, but studying is *not* her strong suit. And that's putting it pretty nicely. When she'd swallowed her food, Lisa mumbled, "Oh, you know, my grades are . . . grades. Um, I really gotta go to the bathroom." She got up from the table and sped out of the kitchen before Mama could question her further. My sister was the queen of wriggling out of sticky situations.

Anyway, by then Mama had gotten up from the table to get a second serving of beef noodle soup. She was no longer listening to either of us.

When Lisa sat back down at the dining table, Mama was still ignoring us to watch YouTube videos on her phone. That was just fine by me. It was better than her interrogating me about my boring school day.

"Winnie, you like to bake, right?" my sister said. Her

eyes met mine across the table. There was a strange, calculating expression on her face—almost like a cat about to corner a mouse.

Uh-oh. That look spelled trouble. I froze, my heart slamming in my chest. Why was Lisa suddenly asking me this question when she *knew* I enjoyed baking yummy treats? She had to have some ulterior motive for bringing this up at dinner. Was Lisa about to expose me for using the oven to bake treats when Mama wasn't home, a.k.a. breaking the rules of the Zeng household? That was so not cool. I thought we'd come to an understanding during the Mid-Autumn Festival and were on better terms now, but maybe it had been a mistake to assume that.

But Lisa just said, "I have to bake cookies for the Key Club's Halloween fundraiser. I need two hundred cookies by the thirty-first. You'll help me out, right, Winnie?"

The forced, too-wide grin Lisa flashed at me said that she wasn't asking me to help so much as she was demanding. Lisa's smile had always been mildly frightening, but now it seemed extra so—because I knew what her words implied. If I didn't help Lisa with this fundraiser, she'd tell Mama about all my rule-breaking baking adventures.

Forget saving Groton from evil spirits. I couldn't even save myself from my blackmailing sister. I guessed that even though Lisa and I seemed to have been getting along recently, old habits were going to die hard.

"You really trust me to make your cookies? What if I mess up?" I asked.

"You won't," Lisa growled, a threatening glint in her eye.

"Fine," I caved. Call me a coward, but I wasn't itching to test Lisa's patience when she was in a mood. Things could be worse. Plus, I didn't mind baking, and I still felt somewhat bad for what I'd done not too long ago, blabbing all about Lisa's secret boyfriend to our parents. Though Lisa and I had made up after the fact, if I helped her make these cookies, then we'd have to be even for sure.

"Thanks." Lisa flashed a genuine smile that somehow scared me even more than her fake one. Then she abruptly stood up.

"You haven't finished your food, Lisa," Mama pointed out, glaring at my sister over the top of her phone.

"Bathroom," Lisa grunted.

"Again? You just went!" I pointed out.

That stopped her for a moment, and she cocked her head to the side, as though she hadn't considered that before. "Did I? I guess I did. Well, there's no law against using the bathroom frequently, is there?" With that, Lisa rushed off to the bathroom again.

I stared after her. She was acting funny. Funnier than usual, I mean. Then again, ever since my sister had started high school, she'd been acting weirder and weirder by the day.

"Look at you and your sister, getting along," Mama said approvingly. She had no idea that Lisa had just blackmailed me right in front of her. Ignorance is bliss.

In the end, I didn't mind that much. Making two

hundred Halloween cookies would be a piece of cake (or cookie, I guess), even if it was for my annoying sister. I just wish she hadn't cornered me into it.

Just then, there came the familiar sound of the garage door opening. Mama and I stared at each other in surprise.

"Your father is home already?" Mama said, slowly setting down her phone. "That's unusual."

When Baba emerged into the kitchen, he looked even more tired than usual. There were huge black circles under his eyes, as though he had barely slept. And had possibly gotten punched in the face at work. His normally neatly combed black hair was sticking up this way and that. Baba always looked kind of tired, but not *this* tired. Work must have been really kicking his butt. Though I was still upset about him backing out of the field trip last minute, another part of me was glad to see my father at a reasonable hour.

"You're home early," observed Mama.

"Am I? What's for dinner?" Baba asked absently. He was really struggling to get his jacket off, trying to pull it over his head without even unzipping it. It was like he'd never taken off a jacket before.

"Beef noodle soup. Um . . . it would help to unzip that," Mama said as she watched Baba struggle with the jacket.

I stifled a laugh. It was pretty funny to see my father, who was always so composed, struggle with something as simple as taking off his jacket. "Um, Baba, do you need help with that?"

"No, I don't need help." With a grunt, my father finally

jerked the zipper all the way down. He yanked it so hard that I was surprised it didn't break. Then he cast off his jacket, flinging it onto the counter as though it had personally offended him. He sniffed the air, and his nose wrinkled in disgust. "Is that beef noodle soup? I don't like beef noodle soup."

"Since when?" Mama asked, raising her eyebrow skeptically. "You always enjoy my beef noodle soup."

Baba's expression turned into a mixture of confusion and disgust. "Oh . . . really?"

"What do you mean, 'Oh, really?'" Mama was looking more and more cross. If I were Baba, I'd be fearing for my life right about now. My mother didn't get angry often, but when she did, she got *furious*. "You said it's your favorite. You always have second or third helpings! Isn't that right, Winnie?"

"Yes," I chimed in immediately. Not that I would have done anything but agree with my mother when she was as ticked off as she was now, but it *was* the truth. Baba really liked beef noodle soup, which was why we ate it at least once a week. I'd never seen him turn down this dish before. Something was off.

Briefly, I thought again about yesterday's news report about the people behaving bizarrely across town. But Baba wasn't behaving *that* strangely. At least he hadn't tried to rob a bank with a carrot. I shook my head. Maybe I was overthinking.

"Well, I'm tired of beef noodle soup now," Baba snapped.

"Oh, you're tired? I'm tired of cooking new food every day." Mama's voice was growing higher and higher pitched, the way it did when she was getting seriously angry. "I have to work, too. So I'm afraid you'll have to put up with my *awful* beef noodle soup."

Work stress often caused my parents to argue over the dinner table, and it was never a good time. I figured we were about three minutes away from a shouting match. Quickly, I gulped down my soup, already planning to use my homework as an excuse to rush back upstairs.

But maybe Baba was too tired to argue, because he just plopped himself down in his seat and began to eat his stew loudly and messily. He splashed his spoon into the soup. I had to duck to avoid getting some of it on me.

Mama's lips scrunched up into a scowl that I recognized as the look she wore before she gave someone an earful. She opened her mouth, and then hesitated, possibly sensing that provoking Baba right now wasn't the best idea. He seemed out of it. Normally, Baba was the neatest eater. The only logical explanation I could think of was that working so much was causing him to lose it. First he'd flaked on my field trip. Now he didn't even like beef noodle soup. I couldn't stay upset at Baba for missing the field trip anymore, because it seemed like he was barely holding it together.

In record time, I finished my food and rushed upstairs. If a fight broke out between my parents, I did not want to be there for it.

CHAPTER NINE

Even though I wasn't making as much progress with catching the class three spirit as I would've liked, there was plenty of other stuff to keep me busy. Halloween was a little more than a week away, and Groton's festivities were in full swing. You could hardly walk down the street without passing by a pumpkin or stepping on a candy corn.

The morning after Baba's weird reaction to beef noodle soup, Mrs. Payton announced that we were going to have a class Halloween party, which sent half the class into wild cheers. Pranav even jumped out of his seat and pounded his fists against his chest, and he's one of the quietest kids in the school. I'm telling you, people around here *really* get into Halloween.

"You'll each be responsible for bringing in one item—treats, napkins, utensils, anything that we need for a party," Mrs. Payton explained. She put a clipboard on the stool in the middle of the room. "I'm going to leave the sign-up sheet here. Let's line up in alphabetical order and write down what we're bringing, okay, class?"

"Are we going to have a contest with Mr. Burnside's class, like we did with the bake sale?" shouted Aiden Chu.

The smile dropped right off Mrs. Payton's face at the mention of Mr. Burnside. It was actually kind of funny how quickly her attitude changed. "Not everything needs to be a competition," our teacher snapped. "We'll be celebrating this holiday together with Mr. Burnside's class." Her teeth clenched when she said the last word, so it came out sounding a lot more threatening than she intended.

"She's still mad about the mayo Mr. Burnside dropped on her at the museum," Melissa Prince said in a loud, carrying whisper. A few people giggled.

"Form a line, now!" ordered Mrs. Payton, and the giggling stopped immediately.

Since the line was in alphabetical order, I ended up being in the very back, after Chika Yamamoto. I was used to it. There weren't many last names that started with Z. In fact, pretty much the only time I wasn't last was when my class did activities with David's. As bad as it was to have a name that started with Ze, Zu was even worse. David could count on being last in alphabetical order for the rest of his life, and probably in the afterlife, too.

Thankfully, the sign-up line didn't take too long. Before I knew it, I was already in front of the clipboard. Everyone else had sat back down at their desks and was packing up to leave for the next class.

Quickly, my eyes scanned the list of items that my classmates had signed up to bring. Napkins, plastic utensils, paper plates, brownies, chips . . . my mouth was watering just looking at this list. I wrote down my name, and the word *cookies* next to it. I hadn't decided yet what kind of cookie I would bring, but whatever it was, it would be delicious.

"Lao Lao! I need your help!"

My grandmother jerked awake from her nap, rubbed her eyes, and stared at me in alarm. She whipped her head back and forth. "What is it, Winnie? Is a spirit attacking?"

"No, nothing like that," I said quickly.

"Oh, then don't *scare* me like that, child. You almost gave me a heart attack." My grandmother made a big, dramatic show of placing her hand over her chest.

"You're dead, Lao Lao," I pointed out. "You can't get a heart attack."

"That's very rude!"

"I need to make cookies for my class next week," I explained. "We're having a Halloween party."

"Halloween," Lao Lao sniffed, as though the word had done something to personally offend her. "What a silly holiday. You know, in Chinese culture, we have a holiday to celebrate and honor the dead, called the Hungry Ghost Festival."

As my grandmother spoke, I sensed a tingling feeling in my gut. It was a feeling that told me something was amiss.

"It's a day to remember our ancestors, not stuff ourselves

silly with candy and cause future cavities," Lao Lao was saying. "And—Winnie, are you listening to me?"

It was rude to leave my grandmother mid-sentence, but I got the unexplainable urge to run downstairs into the kitchen. Something—almost like an otherworldly force—was telling me I needed to be there.

"Winnie, don't run around in the house!" Lisa stuck her head out of her bedroom and frowned at me. My sister looked frazzled. Her normally perfect straight hair was piled up on top of her head in a messy bun, and her pink sweatshirt was all rumpled. She'd been dedicating all her free time to studying ever since her practice SAT scores came back less than stellar. I was pretty impressed by Lisa's commitment to improving her test scores, since I knew how much she hated hitting the books. But I'd never tell her that. Her ego was big enough already. "Are you going to bake something?" Lisa asked sharply.

"Um . . ." Did I have the guilty look of a rule-breaking cookie baker on my face? How had Lisa guessed with one glance?

"You don't get this excited about anything except baking," my sister explained, as though she'd sensed my question before I even spoke it aloud. I swear, even though Lao Lao claimed that our family's shaman powers had skipped over Lisa, she had definitely inherited *some* form of witchcraft. She had a sixth sense for knowing when I was up to something.

"Don't tell Mama," I said. "I have to practice baking cookies to help you with your fundraiser, remember?"

"Yeah, yeah." Lisa waved her manicured nails at me. "Just don't make too big of a mess. And don't be noisy down in the kitchen—I'm concentrating." With that, she disappeared back into her room, shutting the door.

Inside the kitchen, it immediately became clear to me why I'd felt so pulled to come here. One of the drawers—the top one that held all the cookbooks—was *glowing*. I rushed over to the drawer and pulled it open. Lao Lao's cookbook was right on top, and it was the source of the golden glowing light.

"Ah, it appears it is time for you to learn the next recipe, Winnie," Lao Lao said. She and Jade had followed me down the stairs. My grandmother hovered over my shoulder, her face glowing in the light from the cookbook. "That means it's also time to face down our new enemy."

I gulped.

"As you remember from the Mid-Autumn Festival, the mooncake recipe revealed itself to you when the class three spirit Hou Yi had already entered Groton. It is only logical to assume that because the next recipe has unlocked, you're meant to master it to take down your next enemy."

"The class three spirit the Spirit Council warned me about," I murmured.

"Exactly."

I picked up the cookbook and opened it to the mooncake

recipe. Then the page moved—by *itself.* I nearly dropped the book in shock, but I managed to keep ahold of it. An unseen force flipped to the next page, which was a recipe for almond cookies. Then the glow around Lao Lao's cookbook slowly disappeared, until it appeared to be a normal book—minus the fact that when I tried to turn the page, I couldn't. It was stuck fast, as though the remaining pages had been glued together.

I guessed Lao Lao's cookbook was only going to reveal recipes to me one at a time. Honestly, that was probably for the best. The mooncake recipe had only been unlocked when I needed it to fight Hou Yi. I hated to think what would happen if *all* the recipes in this cookbook were unleashed at once. If that ever happened, Groton would be doomed.

"What would happen if all the recipes were revealed at the same time, Lao Lao?" I asked.

"Such a thing shouldn't be possible, given that the magic I cast on the book will only allow the intended user—you— to unlock each recipe as you require it."

"But what if I needed to use all the recipes at once?" I pressed. "Like, what if a bunch of powerful spirits attacked Groton at the same time, and I needed a different power to defeat each of them?"

Lao Lao stared at me with a bemused and mildly concerned look. "By the gods, child, why are you dreaming up the most frightening scenarios?"

I made a face and shrugged. I couldn't help it. Overthinking was my specialty.

Lao Lao pressed her fingers to her temples, as though concentrating hard on the question. At least a solid minute of silence passed before she responded. "If such a thing were to happen—the odds being slim to none—well, if we follow the logic of the cookbook so far, it would mean that many powerful class three spirits had been unleashed upon Groton at once. You'd have to master each recipe to deal with each spirit individually."

So I'd have to bake these treats really, really, *really* fast. "What happens if a new type of spirit enters Groton? One that isn't attached to a recipe in your cookbook?"

My grandmother was silent for a long moment. "In that case, I have . . . I have . . . absolutely no idea what the cookbook would do."

My jaw dropped. "What? How can you have no idea? This is *your* cookbook."

"Well, I didn't account for every hypothetical scenario when I created it," Lao Lao said tersely. "Magic is flexible and adaptable, though, so if such a scenario did occur, I'm sure the cookbook would still make itself useful to you in some way."

"Magic is . . . flexible?" I scrunched up my nose. A funny image of Lao Lao's cookbook doing the splits entered my mind. I couldn't help but giggle, even though I knew she didn't mean *that* kind of flexible.

"Yes," my grandmother was saying, unaware of the silly image in my head. "Though we shamans can learn to control it to some degree, magic obeys its own rules and logic.

Even practiced shamans can't always predict what our magic might do."

In other words, magic could do whatever the heck it wanted. "So . . . you mean to tell me that you can't fully predict your own magic?"

Lao Lao just stared up at the ceiling and whistled, not so subtly dodging my question. It figured. Adults never know the answers to the important questions, like: What is the meaning of life? How are algebra equations going to help us in adulthood? Why can't overspirits predict their own magic, and why do they thrust that responsibility onto their poor unsuspecting granddaughters instead? Very important questions.

I turned my attention from Lao Lao and ran my finger down the recipe for almond cookies, reading the list of ingredients.

Ingredients:

$1\frac{1}{2}$ cups almond flour

Dash of salt

$\frac{1}{2}$ teaspoon baking soda

1 cup unsalted butter

1 cup white sugar (can substitute brown sugar)

2 eggs

2 teaspoons almond extract

Whole almonds

1 packet of fortune

Thankfully, the recipe was simple enough that I could find everything in the kitchen already. The key ingredient—the magical one—was included in the cookbook. A slim red packet labeled with the character for fortune, 福, was pressed between the pages. Carefully, I plucked it out and opened it. It was filled with golden dust.

This almond cookie recipe, I knew, was the key to helping me level up my powers. Baking these cookies would help me get out of my slump, not to mention strengthen my abilities as a shaman. This *had* to be it.

I had already begun adding flour into a big mixing bowl when I heard something that caused my heart to nearly stop: the sound of the garage door opening. I froze, mixer in hand. Oh *no*. Had Mama come home early? She'd be so mad if she saw that I was breaking the rules, making cookies without her supervision. In a panic, I began putting some of the ingredients back into their cupboards, but I wasn't nearly quick enough. The door banged open, and somebody entered the kitchen.

"Winnie?"

I turned around guiltily, surprised that it was not Mama, but Baba standing there. Once again he looked completely worn out, the dark circles under his eyes even darker, if that was possible.

Wait a minute. Why wasn't Baba at the office right now? Especially if he'd been working so much lately that he couldn't make it to my class field trip? I narrowed my eyes, feeling a bit annoyed again. "Why are you home?" I asked, the question coming out more accusatory than I'd intended.

"Work ended early," my father said abruptly. "What are you doing?"

Though I had the sneaking suspicion that Baba wasn't being completely truthful, I decided not to press the matter, especially because he'd just caught me red-handed breaking a household rule—baking without adult supervision.

"Um . . . I can explain," I blurted out. "It's not what it looks like." Of course, it was exactly what it looked like. The ingredients and bowls still piled on the counter could only be used for baking, after all. Hopefully Baba was too tired to put two and two together.

"Looks like you're making something delicious," Baba said with an eager glint in his eye. Instant relief flooded through me. *Phew. He's not thinking straight.* "It's probably much better than that woman's beef noodle soup."

That woman? What had my father just said? My jaw dropped, and for a moment, I was speechless. Baba had never referred to Mama so rudely before. The expression on his face when he said "that woman" was alarming, too. His lips curled into a snarl, making him appear almost frightening. Baba had to be *really* mad at Mama.

"What is it?" my father pressed when I just continued to gape at him.

"Wh-what's what?" I stammered.

The snarl had vanished from my father's face. Now he looked at me with confusion, as though he hadn't said anything out of the ordinary. "The cookies, Winnie. What kind of cookies are you baking?"

"Oh. They're, um . . . they're almond cookies."

"May I have one when they're ready?" Baba asked. "I had to eat leftovers again for lunch today. It was terrible."

Yeah, working all the time was starting to mess with Baba's head. A moment ago he'd had a scary expression on his face, but now he was smiling eagerly. If anything, I would've thought Baba would have been furious with me for breaking the kitchen rules. Though, now that I thought about it, Baba was so rarely around the house that I didn't even know what his thoughts were about me using the kitchen unattended. "Yeah, sure," I finally said, trying not to sound as mystified as I felt. "They'll be ready pretty soon."

"Great. I'll be upstairs sleeping. Save one for me." And with that, Baba turned around and lumbered toward the staircase.

"He seems a little out of sorts, doesn't he?" Lao Lao said once my father had left. She was squinting after him.

"That's for sure." I couldn't put my finger on it, but Baba seemed . . . different somehow. Maybe it was the stress of work. Or maybe it was something else entirely causing his concerning behavior.

"Why do you think that is?"

I shrugged. I didn't spend enough time with Baba to know why he would be acting oddly. And, if I was honest with myself, I was just happy to see him at a regular time, even if I hadn't been all that pleased with him lately. Plus,

Baba wanted to eat one of my cookies! I was really ready to put the field trip behind me and focus on the present.

Now I had to make an extra-tasty batch of cookies. That would be easy. After all, I was Winnie Zeng, and baking was my specialty.

CHAPTER TEN

With Lao Lao's guidance, it didn't take me very long to whip up a batch of delicious, warm almond cookies. The process was a lot simpler than making mooncakes. Though I'd never tried making almond cookies on my own before—and certainly not magical ones—Mama had made them for Chinese New Year parties in the past. The almond cookies are supposed to bring fortune, since they're small and shaped like coins. Chinese people are *big* on symbolism like that. You'd think my luck would be better given how much my parents lean into all that superstition.

After setting aside an almond cookie to give to Baba later, I bit into one of the cookies. It was perfectly flaky and crisp, and not too sweet. The almonds were a little strong, though, and I wasn't the biggest fan of almonds. I'd have to remember to add fewer almonds for next time.

More important, when I bit into the cookie, the warmth that surged into my body wasn't just warmth from the oven. It was magic. A nice, comforting heat rose from the tips of my toes all the way up to the tips of my hair.

"Winnie? Do you feel . . . different?" Lao Lao was staring

at me, wide-eyed, as though she expected me to suddenly begin flying.

I didn't think I'd be flying anytime soon, but I was certain that *something* had changed. As I flexed my fingers, I realized what it was. My senses tingled. This time it was my sense of smell that had sharpened. I could smell the sugar and almonds in the almond cookies much more strongly than before. There were other smells, too. The nail polish Lisa had spilled and valiantly tried to clean off the dining table the other night. The grass on the lawn outside. For a moment, all the smells invading my nostrils were too overwhelming. I had to lean against the wall to steady myself as I adjusted to the newfound intensity of my surroundings.

"Winnie? Are you okay?" Lao Lao asked, concerned.

"Y-yeah, I just . . . wasn't expecting *that*."

"The almond cookies should be giving you a very strong sense of smell," my grandmother said knowledgeably. "In seconds, your body will get used to your newly enhanced senses, and you'll be able to scent what you really need to— the spirit's presence."

My grandmother's words helped calm my racing heart. I took a deep breath in and let it out, repeating a few times. And she was right. After a few more discombobulating moments, I realized the smells had dulled back down, all except for one—a flowery smell. Like what I'd sensed at the Museum of Art History, only stronger and more pungent now. And, furthermore, I could pinpoint the direction it was coming from.

"I . . . I think there's something there, Lao Lao." I turned to my left and stared out of the huge glass door in our dining room, which led out to the patio. There was something rustling in the bushes outside, and it didn't appear to be just the wind.

"Spirits!" shouted my grandmother. "We have to capture them!"

But I was way ahead of her. My feet seemed to be leading the way, before my brain could even catch up with my movement, bringing me closer to that flowery scent. I grabbed a random empty pickle jar from the cabinet. My parents had a habit of collecting and reusing old pickle jars, and I'd never really understood it until this moment. Clearly, they had been preparing me for unannounced evil-spirit attacks.

Pickle jar in one hand, and a few cookies in the other, I ran across the kitchen. I kicked open the sliding door with my foot.

The rustling noise grew louder. And then out of the bush burst a familiar figure.

"H-hello?" I said, flabbergasted.

The mayor of Groton was standing before me, brushing leaves and twigs off his brown suit jacket. I'd never seen Mayor Greene in person before, only on my television screen. He seemed smaller and less impressive-looking in real life. Beside him was a tall, black-haired woman who I recognized as his wife.

"Oh, h-hi, Mayor Greene." I quickly put my pickle jar

behind my back, embarrassed that I'd waved it threateningly at two of the city's most important figures. In my defense, they had done something quite suspicious. Then it finally registered that the mayor and his wife had just casually *emerged from Mama's rosebushes.* If I wasn't careful, my face was going to appear on tonight's news segment, along with Mayor Greene and his wife. "Um . . . are you lost? Do you need help?"

"That's not the mayor, Winnie!" my grandmother shouted. "Look out!"

Mayor Greene's wife started laughing softly, and her body changed. Her skin became transparent, and then red. Two black horns grew out from the top of her head. A split second later, the mayor's skin began to bubble.

I shrieked.

Lao Lao shouted, "Don't be deceived, Winnie. These aren't people. They're evil spirits!"

"I can see that!" The spirits were getting better and better at disguises. I couldn't believe they'd pretended to be Mayor Greene and his wife.

The spirit, formerly Mayor Greene, appeared to be a cross between some kind of demon and a horse. It had horns on its head, with a red face and terrifying fangs, but the body of a horse, almost like a centaur.

"Is it just me, or are these things getting scarier-looking?" I shouted. "What the heck do they feed them in the spirit realm?"

"They're class two spirits. Winnie, your training!" Lao Lao rushed over to my side.

If my powers were ever going to bother working properly again, now was the moment. The spirits advanced on me with a unified roar. Freaking out a bit, I threw a couple of the almond cookies at them. They left burn marks where they hit the spirits' skin, but did little more than annoy them; the spirits batted away the cookies quickly.

"That's not going to work," my grandmother cried. "Look out!"

The red-skinned spirit struck me, its sharp claw scraping my lower arm in a painful swipe. Gritting my teeth, I dove out of the way as the demon-horse spirit rushed toward me.

Lao Lao was right. The almond cookies weren't going to cut it. With two spirits against one shaman, I knew what I needed to do, and I *had* to do it. I had to combine with Lao Lao. And this wasn't like practice, where I could fail over and over and give up. This was the real thing. There was no room for failure.

Concentrating as hard as I could, I dug deep to reach for my power, remembering Lao Lao's training. I tried to clear my mind to unify with my grandmother's spirit. But keeping a clear mind seemed almost impossible—it was as though there were a block in my head, preventing me from forming that telepathic connection with my grandmother. I summoned all my concentration and pushed against it with all my might.

For the space of several heartbeats, nothing happened. Hopeless thoughts filled my head, which was the opposite of what I wanted. Was I going to fail again now, in the critical moment? Was I going to fail to protect myself—and Lisa? What would the Spirit Council say? I imagined the disappointed expression on Jizha's face, and the vindicated one on Zhula's, after I proved her judgment about me correct.

That last part did it. I couldn't *stand* the thought of Zhula gloating because of my failure to perform as a shaman. With another, much stronger mental push, something clicked into place. My mind was able to shove past that block.

I knew I'd succeeded when Lao Lao's voice entered my head, and I sensed her presence in my soul, like a warm embrace.

Good job, Winnie! But don't relax now. The battle has only begun.

I was so focused that I didn't even realize I'd been holding my breath, until I suddenly needed air.

What should we do? I asked my grandmother.

Let me guide you, little one.

The spirits had seemed all too powerful just moments ago. But now, thanks to my combination with Lao Lao, my own abilities were enhanced. My vision was clearer, my sense of smell was sharper, and my body felt light, allowing for faster movement. In comparison, the evil spirits seemed to be moving in slow motion.

There was no time to revel in the elation of successfully combining with my overspirit. In my mind's eye, I could see myself moving. That, I realized, was Lao Lao guiding me—showing me how I could take down these spirits.

Dashing forward, I punched the red-skinned spirit in the jaw. It reeled back. Before it could recover, I gave it a punch with my other hand. Lao Lao's and my combined strength was enough to send the spirit flying backward. As the spirit wailed, it shrank to the size of a peanut, which I captured in the pickle jar.

Winnie, watch out behind you!

I started to spin around. Out of the corner of my eye, I spotted the demon-horse spirit charging at me. My sharpened reflexes kicked in, and I dodged its attack. Kicking off against the ground, I burst toward the spirit to catch it off guard with a punch in the side. Like the other, it cried out, and then began to shrink. I ducked into the kitchen, grabbed another empty pickle jar off the counter, and was back outside in record time. With this pickle jar, I captured the spirit and sealed it inside.

Good girl, came my grandmother's voice of approval.

"Nice," I said, and then Lao Lao's spirit fled my body.

The extra energy from combining deserted me, and I slumped in exhaustion. I could've slept for a million years now. The battle had drained me more than the last time I'd combined with Lao Lao. I wasn't sure why, since last time I'd fought a class three spirit, and these were only class two. Either I really had lost some of my power since the Mid-Autumn Festival, or the spirits were getting noticeably stronger.

The thought was discouraging. How was I supposed to capture spirits and level up fast if they were all getting so much stronger, and so quickly?

I shook my head. There was a more pressing matter that needed my attention—the fact that the mayor and his wife had shown up in my mother's bushes, turned into evil spirits, and attacked me. I wasn't entirely sure what had happened just now, but I knew I needed to check that the mayor was okay. It was already early evening, which meant that Mayor Greene should be on the news soon.

I turned around and rushed into the living room. Quickly, I turned on the TV and flipped to the news channel. There was the mayor, delivering the evening news report alongside Shirley and Jeff. It was very surreal seeing Mayor Greene on the screen, when moments ago he'd been attacking me in my backyard.

"That's so weird," I muttered. The mayor himself seemed to be okay, which begged the question—why had two spirits taken on the form of Mayor Greene and his wife? Had they been planning to cause chaos throughout Groton while in those forms?

"Winnie, are you all right?" Lao Lao peered down at me in concern, then glanced at the TV. "That's the man who the spirit pretended to be, isn't it?"

I nodded. "Yeah, but why go through all the trouble of pretending to be someone else?"

"Perhaps the spirits thought it would be easier to attack you if they seemed more approachable," my grandmother said. "And it seems they were correct. This means we have to have our guard up even higher. The spirits are getting too clever."

"They must be impersonating people all over town!" I gasped as the realization struck me. The woman who'd caused a traffic jam with her inflatable pool, the mailman who was stealing left shoes, the guy who'd used a carrot to try to rob a bank . . . Those hadn't been pranks. Those had been spirits impersonating people, the same way a spirit had pretended to be Mayor Greene—I was almost sure of it. "I need to tell David!" My stomach grumbled, and I realized that defeating those two spirits just now had made me famished. "I think I'm gonna tell David as I finish up these cookies." As I headed back into the kitchen, Lisa came bounding down the stairs.

"Winnie! What was that? I thought I heard something outside the house," she said, leaning against the doorway. She crossed her arms over her chest.

Whoops. Lisa was oblivious, but not *that* oblivious.

"I was . . . baking cookies," I blurted out. Hey, it wasn't a lie. I had been baking almond cookies earlier.

"In our backyard?" Lisa stared over my shoulder at the patio, and then shot me a skeptical look.

"Um, no . . . I dropped a cookie . . . on the patio," I said. Okay, so it wasn't one of my better cover stories, but in my defense, I was coming out of a very stressful situation.

My sister pursed her lips. She clearly didn't believe me. "Whatever," Lisa said finally, and I released a breath, glad that she wasn't going to push it further. "Just . . . don't destroy the house, okay? Otherwise *I'll* get blamed for it." Then she turned around and headed back up the stairs.

After Lisa left, a wave of exhaustion overwhelmed me, and I had to lean against the wall to steady myself.

"Winnie, are you *sure* you're all right?" Lao Lao hovered next to me.

"Yeah, just . . . just catching my breath."

Suddenly I was glad I'd made a whole batch of cookies. I definitely needed something to boost my morale and energy after everything that had happened in the past fifteen minutes.

CHAPTER ELEVEN

The first thing I had to do after capturing the spirits was update David on what I'd learned—plus my accomplishments, of course. And by *update* I mean rub it in his face. I took a picture of the two spirit-filled pickle jars and texted it over to David.

> **Winnie:** Guess who's 2 spirits closer to level one??

> **David:** aw that's cute

> **Winnie:** wdym cute??

> **David:** I've already captured 10 lol

> **Winnie:** liar!!!

> **David:** Nope not lying. Joe and I have been practicing a lot and we can combine like 75% of the time now

Winnie: Show-off . . .

David: Hey, u texted ME to brag

Winnie: also, be extra careful from now on bc the spirits I captured somehow took on the appearance of Mayor Greene and his wife. I think there are spirits impersonating people we know in this town.

David: Wym??

Winnie: You've seen the news reports about ppl doing weird things right? I think that's bc spirits are taking on their appearances and trying to act human but not quite getting it right

David: whoa . . . that makes sense in a scary way. Why are they pretending to be humans tho

Winnie: I wish I knew . . . I guess they think it's easier to defeat us if they trick us at first?

David: yeah ngl I'd prob think twice before attacking the mayor

Winnie: for real tho be careful David

David: Yea yea. I'm still gonna catch more spirits than you tho lol

Annoyed, I left David on read. I didn't think he was exaggerating his spirit-capturing record, either. It would be just like David to casually outdo my accomplishment. Now I really needed to be the one to capture that class three spirit. Someone needed to put David in his place.

"What are you so angry about?" asked my grandmother.

"Nothing," I muttered.

"Good, then wipe that glare off your face."

Oops. I hadn't realized I'd been glaring. Quickly, I plastered a smile on my face.

"Aiyah! Are you trying to scare me now?" Lao Lao gasped, placing a hand over her heart.

I guessed that smile had looked as bad as it felt. "What do you want from me?" I grumbled, my grin slipping.

"That's a better expression." My grandmother nodded in approval.

Now that my heart had mostly settled from the adrenaline rush of what had just happened, I was going over what I'd confirmed with my own eyes. Spirits, likely led by the unknown class three spirit, were disguising themselves among humans. That explained why people were behaving strangely in Groton. And with that knowledge, it became clearer to me that we were dealing with spirits much more clever and capable than the ones we'd dealt with during the Mid-Autumn Festival.

My grandmother was saying, "Next, we have to get these spirits over to the department—"

Before Lao Lao could finish her sentence, a crackling noise came so close to my ear that I nearly jumped. It sounded like a radio. It took me a second to realize that the crackling noise was coming from my badge.

"Winnie? This is Jizha. Can you hear me?"

"Uh, um, yeah, I can! Winnie, at your service." I jumped to a salute before I realized that Jizha couldn't see me. Then I felt very silly, but Lao Lao gave me an encouraging smile.

"The Spirit Council needs your help with an assignment right now. Earlier, we received Xiao Mao's report that an unauthorized portal opened briefly in Groton, which you are aware of, of course. We had warned you that such a thing could—*would*—happen, with spirits moving between realms."

Jizha paused, and it took a moment for me to realize that he was waiting for me to confirm. Tilting my head down, I spoke closer to the badge. "Oh—y-yeah, I know. I was there. At the Museum of Art History."

"Right. Now we've received word that a spirit completely

ransacked the Department of Supernatural Record-Keeping and is currently on the loose."

"What?" That would make it the second time the department had been overturned in a couple months. Considering it was guarded, not to mention located on the eighty-eighth floor, you'd think it would be hard to attack. "Is—is the Suntreader wrecked?"

"No, only the department."

A small wave of relief washed through me, even though the situation was still pretty bad. At least the actual bookstore was okay. The Suntreader had become one of my favorite places to visit. Given how tiny and uninteresting my town was, the Suntreader was pretty much the *only* place I visited often. Groton wouldn't be Groton without it.

"That being said," continued Jizha, "the Department of Supernatural Record-Keeping has suffered significant damage. Given the amount of chaos that has already occurred, in all likelihood this is the work of that class three spirit commanding several lower-level spirits."

"That makes sense," I said as pieces of the puzzle clicked into place. The flowery scent that I'd first encountered at the portal, and then again as I battled spirits outside my home, must have to do with whatever powerful spirit had gotten loose in Groton. That meant I *had* sensed the class three spirit at the museum the other day. "I just captured two class two spirits, and I don't think they were acting of their own accord."

"Well, it's good that you caught them," Jizha said, but he didn't sound all that happy about it. The grave tone of his voice didn't change. "But the fact that the Department of Supernatural Record-Keeping was ransacked is serious, and it cannot be overlooked. The Spirit Council was depending on you and David to protect Groton, and unfortunately, because you failed to stop a rogue spirit from attacking the department, we may have lost highly important records."

With Jizha's every stern word, my stomach sunk lower. My ears burned in shame. Though Jizha didn't say it explicitly, I could read the message behind his words: *You failed at your duty as a member of the Shaman Task Force, Winnie.*

"I . . . I'm sorry," I squeaked out. For a moment, I considered explaining that it wasn't like I'd neglected my duties—I just hadn't sensed or known that a class three spirit was going to wreck the department (and neither had David, for that matter). But that still wasn't an excuse. If I hadn't been able to stop the class three spirit, that meant I wasn't at the level I needed to be yet to safeguard Groton from all spirit attacks.

Jizha continued in slightly less harsh tones, "What's already happened cannot be changed, so we can only move forward and control the damage now. Winnie, your new job is to help clean up the department—and after that, of course, resume your mission. Find and capture that class three spirit, along with any other spirits, and stay on the lookout for unauthorized portals. Are my instructions clear?"

"Yes." I gulped. My mind raced. If a spirit had managed

to overturn the guarded department and was now running about, then it had to be a decently powerful spirit. "Um, about the portal—what does it mean? How did it even open?"

"Right now, we're still trying to figure that out," Jizha explained. "What we know at this moment is that the increasing frequency of portals is a sign of emerging threats. It means that rogue spirits are growing stronger, finding holes between the two worlds, and using them for their own nefarious purposes."

"Fun," I muttered under my breath.

"What was that?"

I cleared my throat. "I said, that's awful."

"Quite. That's why we need you, agent. I expect a report of your success after you've completed this task. Don't make me regret selecting you to join the Shaman Task Force. Good luck." With that, a click sounded from the badge, and Jizha's voice vanished.

Even though I probably could've spent the rest of the week moping over my failure to protect the Department of Supernatural Record-Keeping, there wasn't any time to waste. Trying to ignore the fear that was growing in the pit of my stomach, I glanced over at Lao Lao. "Did you catch all that?"

My grandmother nodded, a small half smile on her face. I didn't know why she'd be smiling when Groton was already in a pinch, until she said, "I'm proud of you, Winnie."

I blinked. I hadn't expected that—not just because my grandmother rarely handed out praise, but also because moments ago Jizha had scolded me for letting the Spirit Council down.

"You're learning to take charge," Lao Lao elaborated. "I can see the makings of a great shaman in you. It's only natural that you'll make a few mistakes along the way, so learn from what happened here, and use that knowledge to become a better member of the Shaman Task Force."

"Th-thank you, Lao Lao. I will." I stood up taller, feeling a little better. If taking my shaman duties seriously meant receiving praise from my grandmother, then I planned to keep doing my best.

"Okay, now that's enough of that," my grandmother said briskly. "You still have to continue proving yourself. Let's get going."

When I arrived at the department, an alarming sight greeted me. Torn papers, which seemed to have been ripped from books, were scattered all around the entrance. The computer appeared to have been flung several feet away from the front desk; it lay in pieces across the room, at the foot of the bookshelves. The area looked like a tornado had blown through it.

Xiao Mao, with help from the Paper Guard, was picking up pieces of paper and stacking them on her desk. Still, there was much more paper on the floor than on the desk. The situation looked hopeless. She glanced up at my arrival and heaved a sigh. "Oh, good. The Spirit Council has sent reinforcements."

"What's going on?" came David's panicked-sounding voice behind me. In moments, he was standing next to me, panting, Joe hovering beside him. I guessed the Spirit Council must have contacted him about the news, too. "What the heck happened here?"

Lao Lao had frozen in shock as she stared at the scene before us. I didn't think I'd ever seen my grandmother so stunned before.

"The Spirit Council contacted me saying that a rogue spirit caused this damage?" I said, though the statement came out like a question.

"Indeed. The department was ransacked overnight. I notified the Spirit Council as soon as I realized what had happened," said Xiao Mao, getting to her feet. The look on her face could only be described as devastation. Her shoulders were slumped in defeat. "I can't believe they got past the Paper Guard. Not *again* . . ."

I glanced over at the Paper Guard. They were holding their paper swords and spears, and turned sideways, so thin that they were nearly invisible. I *could* totally see how intruders would get past the Paper Guard. Actually, I was pretty sure that anyone with a decent right hook—or a sharp pair of scissors, maybe—could take out these guards. But I decided that now wasn't the time to point out the holes in the security. Poor Xiao Mao looked stressed enough already.

"It wasn't our fault," said one of the guards. "The

intruder—it took on your appearance, Xiao Mao. We didn't realize until it was too late."

"Excuses," snarled Xiao Mao. She drew herself up to her full height, which was several feet taller than the guards. They cowered before her. I hadn't realized until now that Xiao Mao could grow so tall. "Get back to cleaning, all of you!" The Paper Guard rushed to obey.

David and I went over to help Xiao Mao clean up the mess. Thankfully, the intruder hadn't really destroyed the room itself—just the books. It was strange that they'd come in and rip apart the books while not really touching the rest of the department, though, like the furniture. Why not destroy everything in the room—unless the culprit had been in search of a specific book?

Wait. The guard's words just now. *The intruder—it took on your appearance, Xiao Mao.* My mind immediately jumped back to what had happened with the two spirits in my backyard.

"I—I think these spirits are learning how to take on others' appearances," I said. The others stared at me. "Earlier today, Lao Lao and I were almost tricked by these two spirits who looked like the mayor and his wife," I explained. "I think it's likely that the Paper Guard really did get fooled by a clever spirit that disguised itself as you, Xiao Mao."

Xiao Mao sniffed and looked away, but didn't say anything.

"If that's the case, we need to be extra careful," Joe said. "Not only are these spirits getting smarter, but they're also harder to detect," Lao Lao said. "I can't always sense the presence of a new spirit. Can you, Joe?" David's overspirit shook his head, and the two overspirits exchanged baffled looks.

"But why are these spirits taking on others' forms?" Xiao Mao mused. "Is it just to trick us?"

Even though I was still feeling pretty bad about having failed to protect the department, hearing that even our overspirits hadn't known what was going on made me feel marginally better.

In the past, when I'd caught loose spirits, my grandmother and I had brought them to the Department of Supernatural Record-Keeping, where Xiao Mao had sent them back into their stories, quite literally. She'd brought out the spirits' storybooks and trapped them inside. I guessed it was only natural that the spirits that had managed to evade capture would come in here to ensure that they wouldn't be captured in the future.

"Are these books . . . repairable?" I asked, staring at the mess of torn pages before me. David slowly gathered up the pages. At this level of destruction, it didn't *seem* possible that those pages could become a book again. But then again, I was still pretty new to all this shaman business. Maybe magic could make these storybooks as good as new.

"Yes, they are," said Xiao Mao. "Though nothing like this has happened under *my* watch before. Throughout history, spirits have gone to great lengths to try to destroy their storybooks—to no avail. In the end, the Department of Supernatural Record-Keeping—and the Shaman Task Force—always prevails." She stood tall and flicked a spot of dust off her shoulder. If she'd had hair, I imagined she would have flipped it back. "However, because the spirits have escaped their stories and are currently up to gods-know-what, that means Groton is at their mercy. The most powerful spirits have been said to be able to put whole towns under their spell."

"Spell?" David squeaked.

"Yes. You, shamans, must be the ones to break this spell by defeating every last spirit and sending them back to their stories." As her heavy words sank in, Xiao Mao blinked at me with her yellow eyes. "Oh, are those for me, dear?"

In all the chaos, I'd nearly forgotten—I'd also brought the two spirits I'd just captured. Holding up a pickle jars, I said, "I've brought two more spirits for you to send back to the spirit realm, but, um . . . is this a bad time?" I felt bad about dumping two more captured spirits on Xiao Mao when she was preoccupied with cleaning up this mess.

"Well, it's not the most ideal time," she sighed, "but I'll take them. Please put them on the desk."

The front desk was covered with so many stacks of paper that I could hardly fit the pickle jars, but I managed somehow. David's eyes followed my movement, and he looked impressed in spite of himself. *Yeah, take that, David.* I'd caught and returned *two* spirits in one day.

"I hope it doesn't take too long to fix those storybooks," Lao Lao said. "Any idea who the culprit might be?"

Xiao Mao shrugged. Then she turned toward me, a grim expression on her face. "That'll be up to the Shaman Task Force to figure out, won't it?"

I suppressed a sigh and exchanged looks with David. Of course. Leave all the difficult tasks to us. But at least more work meant more chances to capture more spirits—and reach level one.

The concerning part was that the ransacking of the Department of Supernatural Record-Keeping had brought up a serious issue: there was a force of evil stronger than the department, maybe even than the Spirit Council, on the loose. And if the shamans didn't stop it—and soon—then we'd be dealing with worse than ransacked departments. According to Xiao Mao, until we captured these spirits, Groton would remain under their spell. No way did I want to find out exactly what *that* meant.

As soon as I left the Suntreader, I tapped my Shaman Task Force badge. Then it occurred to me that I'd never actually called the Spirit Council with it before. Earlier today, Jizha had called me, and I hadn't had to do anything except respond. There weren't any buttons or anything at all on the badge for me to press.

"How do we use this thing?" I asked David, but he was staring down at his badge with an equally mystified expression.

"Um . . . maybe we just speak into it?" Raising his voice, David said, "Hello? Spirit Council?"

A crackling noise, and then Jizha's voice came through

so loud and clear that I had to pull away. "Agents! You were successful, I take it?"

Depended on his definition of *success.* "Well, we helped clean up the department," I said, "but whatever spirit caused this chaos in the first place is long gone, and we don't know where it is now."

"Xiao Mao didn't seem to know anything about it, either," David added.

"We did learn something important, though." I recounted the situation with the spirits disguising themselves as Mayor Greene, his wife, and Xiao Mao.

There was a long silence at the other end after I finished my explanation. I braced myself for Jizha to lecture us about being tricked by spirits, plus about not having captured the spirit responsible for messing up the department records. Instead he released a long sigh, which caused more feedback and forced me to pull away from the badge again.

"Well, that's unfortunate," said Jizha. "I'm afraid your job won't be done until you've captured the culprit. As for the reason why spirits are disguising themselves as humans— well, that's an indication that they're growing more powerful and daring, and must be rounded up by Halloween, before they can cause greater destruction. Do your best, agents. Until then, if you ever need to reach the Spirit Council, just call again."

"Wait, but can't you give us a clue or anything about this spirit?" I blurted. "Hello?"

But there was no longer any crackling to be heard, and Jizha didn't respond. David just looked at me and shrugged. I guess the call had ended. And once again, David and I were on our own to do all the dirty work.

We headed to David's house to regroup after what had happened at the Department of Supernatural Record-Keeping. I could tell everyone was shaken by the incident, because we were all quiet on the way over. Lao Lao and Joe didn't exchange a single insult. That's how I knew this matter was *very* serious.

As soon as we entered his house, David let out a long-suffering sigh. Then he sank down into his couch, deeper and deeper until he was practically buried in the cushions.

"You good, David?" I said.

"I've been better," he murmured. "Like, a few hours ago, before I knew what happened at the department, I was better." His eyes grew wide, and he suddenly sat up. "What happens if the Spirit Council isn't able to fix all those storybooks?"

We both looked toward Lao Lao and Joe. But the spirits' faces were blank. They shook their heads. It was the first time I could remember seeing them in unison.

"That would be terrible, if those storybooks remained ruined." Joe shuddered. "Those stories would simply be lost forever. And all the while those spirits would be feeding off the chaos on Earth, growing more powerful. They'd do despicable things, like put pineapple on pizza."

"*No,*" David gasped.

I frowned. "What's wrong with pineapple on pizza?"

Joe and David gave me a horrified look that really emphasized the family resemblance. Before either could say a word—and before I could defend pineapple pizza—Lao Lao interrupted. "Can we get back on topic, please? The destruction of the storybooks?" she prompted.

"Right," Joe muttered.

"I think it's likely that—" David started, but was interrupted by the sudden buzzing of our badges.

I jumped a little in shock. The badges really did function like radios—very advanced radios. A voice came through, sounding as clear as though the speaker were standing right next to me.

"This is Jizha," said the voice. "The Spirit Council had a meeting just now, and we unanimously voted that you two actually *do* need help, as the situation at the department has shown that the strength of two isn't enough. Effective immediately, we're dispatching emergency help to Groton. A level one shaman will be joining your ranks by tomorrow morning."

David stared at me, and I shrugged. But the implication in Jizha's words was clear. The Spirit Council was sending backup to Groton because David and I weren't good enough to protect the town on our own. I couldn't exactly *dis*agree with that, which was the worst part. After all, if David and I had been skilled enough to protect Groton without outside help, then the Department of Supernatural Record-Keeping wouldn't have been attacked with Halloween just days away—or, at the very least, we would've sensed the spirit responsible for the mess. It only made sense to send over another, more skilled shaman. If David and I couldn't prevent an attack like that before Halloween, then how were we going to handle the influx of evil on Halloween night?

Still, I wanted to protest, but I forced myself to swallow my pride. It was only natural for the Spirit Council to send reinforcements.

"Who is it?" asked David. He looked grumpy. Clearly, I wasn't the only one whose pride had been wounded.

"I expect you'll find out tomorrow morning," Jizha said mysteriously.

"Or you can just tell us and we can find out right now," David muttered under his breath so that only I could hear him.

"Until then, try not to let any more foul spirits run amok, please."

"It's not like we *allowed* that mess to happen," I blurted before I could stop myself. Not that it mattered. There was no response, except the sound of static, and then silence. Jizha had gone. Now all there was left to do was wait and see who the Spirit Council had sent to Groton as backup.

CHAPTER TWELVE

We didn't have to wait long to find out the identity of the new shaman in town. The next day, during PE, Mr. Nichols announced that we had a transfer student.

"This is Kelly. Kelly Mayo," he said, patting the shoulder of the new girl.

"Miao," she corrected.

"Exactly. Mayo."

"Miao," Kelly insisted, but the teacher seemed not to hear her.

"Kelly transferred to us from Chicago. It's quite a transition, going from the big city to our small humble town. So let's do our best to welcome her, all right?"

Kelly was a tall girl with big brown eyes and shoulder-length, straight black hair that had a white headband in it. She wore shiny pink lip gloss, and her nails were painted pink. Her dress was pink, too. She looked like she'd fit right in with the popular girls, Tracy, Kim, and Jessamyn. She looked *nothing* like a shaman. Well, I wasn't certain what shamans were *supposed* to look like, but pink on pink wasn't the first color scheme to come to mind. But if the new shaman wasn't Kelly, who'd transferred here on the same day the Spirit Council said our reinforcement would arrive, then who else could it be?

"Hey, Kelly! Come join our group." It was Jessamyn, waving Kelly over to join her, Tracy, and Kim. Today was free day in gym class, which meant we could choose to play whatever sport we wanted. Jessamyn and her friends had grabbed a volleyball and were tossing it around. Tracy caught my eye and gave a small smile. Though I wasn't exactly friends with the popular girls, we were pretty cordial. I'd helped save Jessamyn when the presence of Hou Yi's spirit had been freezing residents of Groton.

"No, thank you," said Kelly curtly, turning away from Jessamyn. "I have a mission."

There was a chorus of gasps. Nobody ever turned down an invitation from the popular girls. Also, what a weird phrase she'd used to turn them down. What did Kelly mean by "a mission"? A *shaman* mission?

Jessamyn stood there with her jaw slightly dropped, eyes practically popping out of her head in shock. Her cheeks turned redder and redder. Clearly she hadn't even entertained the possibility that Kelly would shut her down. As I said, nobody turned down the popular girls—nobody who cared about their social standing, anyway. And Kelly really looked like she'd fit right in with the trio.

Though the whole situation was pretty funny, I didn't dare to laugh. I still cared about my social standing, and I did not want to be on the trio's bad side again.

Veronica Beauman scrambled to her feet. "I'll play volleyball with you guys," she volunteered, and flashed a too-eager smile at the three girls, showing off her braces.

"Go away, Veronica," snapped Jessamyn.

Things got even stranger when Kelly walked away from the popular girls—and made a beeline for David and me. We'd congregated near the stairs of the bleachers, far away from our gym teacher, hoping he wouldn't notice that we weren't using the jump ropes we'd brought with us. Mr. Nichols was currently yelling at a group of boys for using the yoga mats to whack each other. Yeah, he was going to be preoccupied for a while.

"That's her, isn't it?" David said, biting his lip. I guess even David got intimidated sometimes. "Kelly. The reinforcement sent by the Spirit Council."

"Yeah, looks like it."

"Hmmm." David's expression was hard to read, but from the way his eyebrows pulled together, I could tell he was assessing her—and doing his best to dislike her.

When Kelly reached us, she crossed her arms over her chest and cocked her head to one side, studying us. I didn't like that look on her face. It reminded me of how Jessamyn sized up other girls before she lobbed a mean comment about their clothes or makeup. Now that Kelly was so close to us, I could see there was a shiny bronze badge affixed to her dress. She was *definitely* a member of the Shaman Task Force.

"You two," Kelly said abruptly. "You're Winnie and David, right?"

We nodded, too surprised to do or say anything else. How had Kelly been able to single us out in an instant?

"This is what the Spirit Council assigned to Groton?" she said, and not in a very nice way. "No wonder this town needs my help."

I narrowed my eyes. I'd been willing to reserve judgment on Kelly, but now I felt like David had the right idea. "Excuse me?"

"You two are the rookiest-looking rookie shamans ever." Kelly raised her eyebrows as she looked us up and down. And I definitely wasn't imagining that she emphasized the word *rookie*. I couldn't wait to level up and make sure nobody could refer to me like that again.

"What does a rookie even look like?" I grumbled.

"Wait, and how could you tell that we're . . . *you know what?*" David lowered his voice and glanced around. We were attracting stares, thanks to Kelly. It was pretty bold of her to start talking about shamans while our classmates were watching us.

"You mean you two can't just tell shamans apart from regular humans?" Kelly said haughtily.

What was up with this girl's condescending attitude? I opened my mouth heatedly, ready to let her have it. I wasn't sure what I would say, but I knew it would be good.

"I'm kidding," Kelly continued. "The council showed

me pictures of you two before I arrived. Also, your badges are a dead giveaway. Duh."

David let out a short, uncomfortable laugh that quickly stopped. It took me a minute to realize that Kelly had attempted a joke. She had a weird sense of humor.

"How long are you in Groton for?" I asked. *Please say you're leaving by lunchtime. Please oh please oh please.*

Kelly smiled, flashing perfectly white teeth. "I'm staying here until I get reassigned."

"And . . . when would that be? Next week?" David said hopefully.

She shrugged and examined her cuticles. "Oh, judging by how much help Groton needs . . . probably a decade at least."

Great.

When the Spirit Council had assigned Kelly to us, apparently they'd meant to make sure all three of us shamans stuck together all day. Unfortunately, Kelly ended up being in my homeroom, plus all my classes except one—Mrs. Lee's English class.

We had a substitute teacher in English today, Mr. Nguyen. He put on the movie *Remember the Titans* and then ignored us to do stuff on the computer. That basically gave us a free hour, so David and I congregated in the back to "get a head start on homework."

"Kelly's awful," David grumped as soon as I pushed a desk next to his. "We've got to get rid of her."

"How?" I whispered, glancing around to make sure nobody was eavesdropping. Everyone was too wrapped up in their own conversations, or sleeping. Mr. Nguyen was now too busy with his phone to notice that none of us were paying attention to the movie. "It sounds like the Spirit Council wants to keep her here for a long while."

"We'll have to convince them that we don't need Kelly. That means you need to step up your game, Winnie."

I gritted my teeth. "Me? What about you? If you're so great, why did the Spirit Council send Kelly anyway?"

For once, David didn't seem to have a comeback. Instead he sighed, appearing to deflate, his shoulders slumping. We both knew exactly why the Spirit Council had sent Kelly.

"Never mind," I said. Arguing with David was pointless. It didn't matter who could one-up the other. We had to focus on the two big problems at hand—protecting Groton from evil spirits, and making sure Kelly didn't overstay her welcome.

"Are we really doing *that* poor a job protecting Groton?" David grumbled. "*I* don't think so."

I thought back on the events that had happened since I had unlocked my shaman powers. A bunch of people had been frozen in Groton, the Suntreader was thrown into disorder, the Department of Supernatural Record-Keeping had been totally ransacked, and now there were more evil spirits on the loose, who-knew-where, doing gods-knew-what.

"Well . . . you know, at least the town is still standing," I offered, and then, thinking that was too generous, I added, "Mostly." Yes, the town was standing, but it had definitely had a close call when Hou Yi had been on the loose, freezing residents.

David banged his forehead against his desk. "Kelly is right. We're gonna be stuck with her for a decade."

I kept a close eye on Kelly throughout the rest of the day. To my dismay, the teachers *loved* her. Of course they did. In math class, Kelly raised her hand to answer almost every question, and she got them all correct. It was as if she was going out of her way to prove how much more advanced she was than everyone else in the class.

The more Kelly stood out in school, though, the less popular she became. By offending Jessamyn earlier, Kelly had pretty much doomed herself to social-outcast status. By the end of the day, Jessamyn had made sure that nobody would talk to Kelly. Kelly didn't seem to care about what was going on, though. I didn't know where this girl got so much confidence from, but it was actually pretty admirable.

When the final bell rang to signal that the school day was over, Kelly swung her black backpack over her shoulder and strutted straight out of the classroom, totally unbothered by the death glare Tracy was sending her way.

"Chicago kids are built different," I heard Jeremy whisper to Pranav.

When I headed outside, I went straight for the bike rack, but then a shadow fell over me as I was unlocking my bike. I startled and looked up to find Kelly.

"Oh, um, hi," I said. "You rode a bike too?"

"My daddy is picking me up," said Kelly, tossing her hair over her shoulder. She pointed behind her, where there was a black Toyota Camry lined up between buses. "I just wanted to let you know that I caught a class one spirit earlier today. It was behind the school." She raised something in her left hand—a mason jar.

I gaped. "What? When did you do that?" I'd been watching Kelly almost all day, and I would've noticed if she'd gone and taken down a freaking spirit in the middle of class. At least, I hoped I would. Did Kelly do it during math class when I briefly fell asleep?

"During lunch. You have to be more vigilant, even with low-level spirits. How did you and David even catch any spirits before I got here?" She wrinkled her nose.

"David and I were managing just fine," I said sourly. Okay, maybe I was stretching the truth a little, but we *had* been able to defeat evil spirits when it really mattered.

"Oh, really?" Kelly scoffed. I sensed even ruder remarks coming from her and braced myself for a verbal match. But, just then, Kelly's dad honked the car horn really loudly, interrupting whatever she was about to say. Everyone within a fifty-foot radius turned around to stare. Kelly rolled her eyes and mumbled something that sounded like "Ugh, so embarrassing." Then she gave me one last frown. "Okay, give me your number."

"What?"

"Your number," Kelly repeated slowly. "So I can keep in contact with you in case of emergencies."

Giving Kelly another means of communicating with me was the last thing I wanted to do, but it would probably be rude to turn her down. So I sighed and recited my phone number, which she saved onto her pink phone. Then she turned toward her dad, who honked the horn again. "Coming, Dad! I'll see you tomorrow, Winnie."

All the way home, I couldn't shake off Kelly's words, nor the snooty expression she'd worn on her face. How dare Kelly flounce into Groton and look down on the work that David and I had done? Okay, so I'd never been that fired up about my shaman duties before I received my shaman badge, but there was no way I'd back down and take Kelly's attitude like this.

As soon as I got home, I ran up the stairs and headed straight for my room. Lao Lao was fast asleep next to Jade's cage. I flung myself on my bed, opening my texts to message David.

> **Winnie:** Kelly just told me she captured a class one spirit that was lurking behind our school today!!

David: She's gotta be lying, I didn't sense anything

Winnie: She's not. She showed me the captured spirit. At this rate she's def going to make us look bad 😫 Not to mention she'll capture all the spirits before we can get to them . . . how are we ever gonna level up?

David: Ok so we just gotta improve our skills until we're better than her

Winnie: . . . you make it sound so easy

David: It will be for me, idk about you

Winnie: Wowwwww thanks.

David: Anytime 😊

Winnie: Any chance you got time to train today?

David: Nah I gotta go to piano lessons tonight

> **Winnie:** Spirit hunting >>>>>>>>>>>>
> piano

> **David:** Tell that to my mom lol

With a sigh, I tossed my phone to the other end of my bed. David had piano lessons, and no doubt Kelly was excelling at her own form of training. Meanwhile I was just lying here like a lump in my bed. I knew I should practice piano, too, even though I didn't have any competitions or recitals coming up (for once).

As I was trying to settle on what to do, my phone buzzed. I quickly picked it up to see that I'd received a text from a new number. There was a photo of a mason jar with the essence of a spirit inside.

> **555-667-0891:** Spirit number two today ☺

I flung my phone across the room.

CHAPTER THIRTEEN

"Seriously, why did the Spirit Council have to assign a freaking *genius* shaman to our town?" David grumbled.

It was Sunday. We were sitting in our Chinese school classroom waiting for class to begin. I was ready to go home already and sleep for a million years. It had been a very, very long week at Groton Middle School. Turned out that not only was Kelly a top-notch member of the Shaman Task Force, but she was also a top-notch student in every class. Which was totally unfair. How could one person find the time to excel at so many things? I sure couldn't. My grades had started dipping ever since I'd taken up my responsibilities as part of the Shaman Task Force.

"Look, I'm not a fan of her either, but I understand why the Spirit Council sent Kelly to help us," I sighed. "The evil-spirit situation here wasn't exactly improving at rapid speed, even with us two trying our best. And Kelly is . . . well, she definitely knows what she's doing." I couldn't believe these words were coming out of *my* mouth, but after days of witnessing Kelly prove why she was every parent's dream child, I had to admit that everyone in Groton was in better hands with Kelly here.

Kelly had spent the rest of the week volunteering to answer teachers' questions in every class. She got them all right, too. By Friday, all the sixth-grade teachers loved her—even the PE teacher, and he didn't like *anyone*. Too bad the students didn't share that feeling. Snubbing Jessamyn's group on the first day had been a *really* bad move. But, then again, it didn't seem like Kelly cared that much. When the girls laughed meanly in the hall as Kelly passed by, she just kept her eyes glued straight ahead and walked like she couldn't hear them or didn't care. If anything, I felt worse for Kelly than she did for herself.

Anyway, at least I'd had a somewhat relaxing Saturday without seeing Kelly at all, and I was hoping Sunday would pass by peacefully, too. As long as Chinese school went without a hitch, and as long as I didn't have to see—

"Kelly?" David stood up so fast that his chair clattered to the floor. He gaped at the doorway. I turned toward where David was looking, my stomach dropping with dread. I already knew what I was going to see.

Sure enough, standing in the doorway was none other than . . . Kelly Miao. Because of course. In hindsight, I should have expected this. There was only one Chinese school in the whole town, after all.

Kelly was wearing a black shirt with an anime design on it that I recognized from *Demon Slayer*, even though I'd never watched the anime myself. As much as she could dress fashionably for school, I guess she could dress comfortably, too. She was stony-faced as per usual, though. Kelly's eyes narrowed a bit when they landed on David and me, the only indication that she recognized us.

"Wh-what are you doing here?" I spluttered.

"Attending Chinese school, duh." Kelly made her way across the room and dropped her blue backpack on the desk next to mine with a thud. The chair scraped as she pulled it back and then sat in it. "Why? Are you here for something else?"

"No, I mean—this—I—This is *my* Chinese school," I said.

"Ours," David coughed.

I continued, "You're invading New Chapter Chinese School too?"

She glared. "I am not *invading*. My parents signed me up for the nearest Chinese school. It's not like this school belongs to you." When I didn't reply, Kelly settled further into her seat, a satisfied look on her face. Then she snapped at David, "You got something to say to me, too, David?"

He blinked. "Oh, no, I just, um . . . nice shirt. I like *Demon Slayer*, too."

Kelly smiled a real, genuine smile, for the first time since I'd met her. "It's a great show. Very educational, especially for, you know, people like us."

"Yeah, and the action is really— *Ow!*"

I'd elbowed David in the rib cage. As he rubbed the spot, shooting me an annoyed look, I tried to convey my message with my eyebrows alone: *Stop fraternizing with the enemy.*

"Whoa, Winnie, your eyebrows are seriously out of whack," he said, giving me a look of concern. "You good?"

I rolled my eyes. It was too bad David had only developed the power to see spirits, not to read the room.

More of my Chinese school classmates trickled in, some of them throwing curious looks at Kelly. Allison Tan, one of the other kids who attended Groton Middle School, sat down hesitantly next to Kelly, who'd taken her usual spot.

"Oh, hey. Kelly, right?" said Allison.

"Hey, Allison." Kelly tapped her bottom lip as she stared at Allison's mouth. "Is that ColourPop you're wearing?"

"Yeah!"

Just like that, the two girls struck up a conversation, something about Allison's pink lip gloss. David and I looked at each other and shrugged.

Mrs. Lin, our teacher, hurried in a few minutes after the bell had already rung, her hair practically falling out of its loose ponytail. Mrs. Lin was always running at least fifteen minutes late, rushing about from here to there in a sweaty mess. Just watching her was enough to make me anxious.

"Class, we have a new student joining us today," said our teacher after she'd caught her breath. Everyone turned around to stare at Kelly, who gave a tight-lipped smile and a small wave. It was a small class, only fifteen of us in total, so it was pretty obvious who the new student was. If I were Kelly, I'd be sick of getting stared at by now. But maybe she liked the attention. "This is Miao Peilin."

I hated to admit it, but Kelly's Chinese name had a nice ring to it.

After that, Mrs. Lin dove right into collecting last week's homework and getting started with this week's lesson. We were learning about Chinese idioms. Idioms are usually four characters long, which should make them easy to re-member, except the meaning is always super philosophical and impossible to understand. I'm pretty sure the ancient scholars were just yanking people's chains when they came up with these expressions, except everyone took it seriously and now they've made students memorize these phrases for generations. Thanks a lot, scholars.

As our teacher lectured, my mind wandered away from the day's lesson. Keeping up with Chinese school suddenly didn't seem as important as tracking down and capturing this pesky class three spirit, not to mention the other spir-its that had been popping up in Groton. I couldn't wait for school to be over so I could go home and keep training with Lao Lao.

"So, class, can anyone tell me what this idiom means?" asked Mrs. Lin, pointing at four characters that she'd writ-ten and underlined on the board.

It took me all of two seconds to read and register the characters: 全心全意. In that time, Kelly's hand shot up into the air like a rocket, nearly clipping my ear in the process.

"Hey," I muttered, frowning. Kelly didn't seem to notice.

"Yes, Peilin?" said the teacher, her expression both surprised and delighted.

Kelly stood up to answer the question, clearing her throat in a confident manner. (I didn't even know before this moment that one could clear one's throat *confidently*, but Kelly managed this.) "Quán xīn quán yì," she said, reading with what the teacher would have described as "flawless pronunciation." "It means to do something with your whole heart."

"Very good." Mrs. Lin brought her hands together and clapped a couple of times. "The Chinese school you attended back in Chicago must have been excellent, hmm?"

Kelly tucked her hair behind her ear, her nose high up in the air. "It was number one in the state."

Of course.

David and I looked at each other. He'd half risen out of his seat in his eagerness to answer the question, and now slowly sat back down with a disappointed look on his face. Before Kelly's arrival, David had been the unspoken brownnoser and top student of the class. Maybe David could tolerate Kelly outshining him at capturing spirits, but I knew his ego wouldn't stand for her showing him up in Chinese school, too.

As for me? Kelly taking the top spot here meant *I'd* been knocked down a peg as well. I was probably the third or fourth best student now, depending on if Allison Tan was having a particularly good day or not. I had a feeling that

Chinese lessons would proceed much the same way that our Groton Middle School classes had—with Kelly effortlessly claiming the top spot.

By the time the recess bell rang, Kelly had answered the teacher's questions correctly three more times, and Mrs. Lin practically got stars in her eyes when she looked at Kelly. I checked my phone as I got up to leave the classroom. There was a missed text notification from Lisa.

Lisa: Meet me in the courtyard when you receive this note.

Quickly, I wrote a reply. Lisa did *not* like to be kept waiting.

Winnie: K I'm omw now

Lisa: Excellent.

Tilting my head to the side, I studied the text. Something about it was odd. Why was Lisa texting all formal, with periods and everything? Was she mad at me? I hadn't done anything to her lately, so I didn't see why she would be. And why did she refer to her text message as a "note"?

Whatever—I didn't have time to dwell on a few odd texts. I rushed out of that classroom faster than Kelly could answer a teacher's question, with David right on my heels.

The halls of the community college soon filled with Chinese school students as young as five to as old as eighteen, as we took our one-hour break from class.

"I can't believe that Peilin—I mean Kelly," David muttered as we sidestepped a group of kindergartners who were running down the hall. "There's no way she can be this good at *everything*. She doesn't have any weaknesses, and it doesn't make sense! It isn't *fair*."

"David, you're just salty that you're not the favorite student anymore."

"Of course I'm salty! You wouldn't get it. You've never been the favorite student." He lengthened his strides to keep up with me. "Why are you in such a hurry, anyway?"

"I'm going to meet my sister," I said as we drew closer to the exit door that led to the courtyard. "You don't have to follow me. In fact, please don't."

Before David could reply, a scent wafted into my nostrils—that familiar, vaguely flowery smell I'd detected at the museum when the portal opened. In a moment, I understood what was happening.

I whirled around and hissed, "David. There are spirits nearby."

"What? How do you know?" David's eyes widened, and he whipped his head back and forth.

"Do you smell that?"

He sniffed the air. "Smells like . . . chalk? And sadness."

"No, not the school smell. There's another smell, like—like—"

"Flowers," David murmured, eyebrows scrunching together.

I nodded. "The flowers. That's what I smelled back at the museum, when that portal opened."

David's jaw dropped. "So you think that this flowery smell means the spirits are nearby?"

"It can't be a coincidence." At least, I didn't want to believe it was a coincidence. This might finally be a lead, some knowledge that we had—and Kelly didn't. If I was right, then evil spirits were stirring near New Chapter Chinese School once again, and *we didn't have our overspirits with us.*

"What do we do?" I blurted out in panic. The Chinese school was way too far from my house for me to make a quick trip to pick up Lao Lao and then come back. Ugh. Why hadn't I thought to plan ahead and bring my grandmother with me? Yeah, it would have been annoying figuring out how to sneak a rabbit into the Chinese school—last time I'd attempted that, things had gone south *fast*—but at least it would've been worth the hassle for this moment.

David opened his mouth to reply but got interrupted by a shout.

"Hey, David! Winnie!" Kelly was running down the hall, waving at us.

"There's no time to waste," said David, his eyes scanning the area.

"You both sensed this spirit, too, right? Feels like it's coming from the side exit." Kelly pointed down the hall, toward the exit that led to a small courtyard outside the building.

At first I was stunned that Kelly had, once again, been able to locate the presence of a spirit so quickly. Even though I thought David and I had this one over her, she'd proven yet *again* how capable she was.

But before I could get too annoyed by that thought, another, more horrifying thought struck me. "My sister is out there in the courtyard waiting for me!" I blurted, then covered my mouth with my hand. Lisa had already been attacked and frozen by spirits during the Mid-Autumn Festival. No way could I let her get hurt again. "Wh-what should we do?"

"Our overspirits aren't here," David blurted to Kelly. He spoke too loudly, and the nearest group of students—high schoolers, judging by their height and bored-to-death expressions—gave us a funny look. But I couldn't care about that right now. This was an emergency.

"You didn't bring your overspirits?" Kelly rolled her eyes. "Juvenile error."

"It's against the rules to bring pets to school," I said through gritted teeth. "Technically, you're breaking the rules!"

Kelly snorted. "Of course I didn't have to bring a pet. My overspirit and I are so in tune now that I don't need an animal anchor. That's what happens when you level up your powers. See?" She snapped her fingers. An instant later, the silvery, ghostly figure of a tiny old woman appeared at Kelly's shoulder. She looked like she'd rolled right out of bed into Chinese school. She wore a thick bathrobe and fuzzy slippers. "This is my Nai Nai," Kelly said, which I knew meant her paternal grandmother.

"What's this?" said Kelly's grandmother, peering down at us from beneath her half-moon spectacles. She gave us a kind smile. It was hard to see the resemblance between her and Kelly, who was currently glaring at us. "More shamans, Kelly? Introduce me."

"Yes, they're shamans, but their names don't matter."

"Hey!" David protested.

"Don't matter *at the moment*," Kelly clarified. "There's no time for introductions right now. We're sort of having an emergency, and we need your help, Nai Nai."

"Well, then, let's not waste a second," said Kelly's over-spirit.

Kelly zipped open her backpack and dug through it. She pulled out a pencil case, folders, books . . . and, finally, a red fan with gold flowery decorations on it.

"Oh, I have one of those, too!" I said. Back in second grade, Mama had signed me up for the Chinese school's dance team, and we'd used fans just like that.

"You . . . you are going to fan the spirit?" David said, staring at the fan blankly.

"Are you a shaman or not?" Kelly demanded, losing her patience. "This fan is the source of my power. I use it to dance, and the more complicated the dance, the more power I obtain. Thankfully, I prepared before Chinese school *just* in case, so I still have plenty of power." She began twirling the fan, flicking her wrists and executing pretty complicated-looking movements. David and I stumbled back, giving Kelly a wide berth.

As Kelly moved, I looked at the fan, and noticed that it seemed to be faintly glowing with power. The glow grew stronger with each of her motions, and it traveled from Kelly's fingertips through her body. Just like Lao Lao's recipe book was the source of my power, and calligraphy was the source of David's, the red-and-gold fan was the source of Kelly's.

"I'm ready. Let's get going!" Kelly said after another moment passed.

The three of us raced down the hall and toward the side exit. But there was somebody blocking our path—a bald-headed, stocky man with a scruffy black beard, who I recognized as Vice Principal Guo. At the sight of us, he frowned and crossed his arms over his chest, blocking the exit.

"There's no running allowed in these halls," scolded the vice principal. "You've broken the rules, children."

"Sorry, Mr. Guo, but we're in kind of a rush," I explained, craning my neck to try to see behind him. As far as I could tell, there was nobody outside in the courtyard—no Lisa, and certainly nothing that resembled an evil spirit.

But Vice Principal Guo didn't seem inclined to accept my apology, nor let us past him. "Rule-breakers need to be punished," he growled, his voice a much lower timber than

I remembered. Also, was it my imagination, or did his arms and legs appear bulkier, with more muscles, than before?

"Wait—you're not Mr. Guo!" I shouted, the truth clicking.

"You're not even a man!" Kelly accused.

My body was faster to react than my mind, which was still processing the fact that once more an evil spirit had fooled us by disguising itself as a human.

Mr. Guo sneered. "Slow on the uptake, aren't you, little shamans?" His appearance began melting and bubbling.

Thinking fast, I flung open the side-exit doors. "Come and get me, nasty spirit!" I yelled. If we could get the evil spirit outside into the empty courtyard, at least there'd be no chance of putting others in danger as we fought it.

Luckily, my plan worked. The spirit, which looked like a terrifying, melted Mr. Guo at this point, roared and charged after me. David and Kelly followed on its tail. I ducked around a huge oak tree, and the spirit tripped over a couple of lawn chairs. That gave me a moment to catch my breath.

"Good thinking, Winnie," panted David, who'd ducked behind the tree with me.

"Don't let your guard down just yet," I warned. The formerly Mr. Guo spirit had reverted back to its true form—that of a deer. And not a friendly one. When it caught sight of us behind the oak tree, the spirit charged, and it charged *fast*.

"Careful, guys!" Kelly bellowed from the other side of the courtyard. "This one's quick! Let me handle it. I'm the only one with the overspirit."

I dove behind a nearby bush to get out of the spirit's path. When I looked back, David had grabbed a fallen tree branch and was waving it threateningly at the spirit. I grabbed one, too, to help back him up, while Kelly held her fan up high in the air. The magical glow around the fan grew brighter, traveling down Kelly's arms and the rest of her body, until it encased all three of us in a warm golden light.

Then Kelly's overspirit combined with her in a burst of light. It happened so quickly that I hardly registered what had happened until it was over. For a second, I just stood there in awe. Kelly really was on a whole different level from David and me. I hadn't even known it was possible to combine that fast.

"Look out!" I shouted.

The spirit, undeterred, charged forward once more— but stopped in its tracks as soon as it reached the wall of golden energy. The spirit let out a wail and stumbled back. Where its body had touched the energy, angry red scorch marks appeared. It tried to advance again, but again it was burned. Each time it got burned, the spirit shrank in size.

It seemed that Kelly's fan and overspirit had given us protection from the spirit's attack. But I wondered how long that protection would last. Already the golden glow was wavering, and Kelly's face was turning red from the effort.

"What can we do to help?" David cried.

"Capture ... the spirit ... ," she managed to say through gritted teeth.

Still holding the tree branch in my right hand, I reached into my backpack with my left, grateful that I'd at least thought to bring a mason jar with me to Chinese school. At the same time, David and I stepped out of Kelly's protective glow. Our eyes met. I didn't know how, but I could tell exactly what David was thinking when he nodded at me. I guess we'd worked together enough now that I could sense what was on his mind. And besides, after years of trying to one-up David, I knew him probably better than he knew himself.

One of us—I—would distract the spirit, and the other— David—would sneak up and attack it.

The spirit was smaller now, but not so small that I could easily trap it in the mason jar. When its eyes landed on me, I swear they grew redder, and it bared its fangs. The spirit lunged toward me, taking its eyes off David. I turned and ran. Moments later, the spirit's shrieks filled the clearing.

David had whacked it with the tree branch. The spirit let out a howl, falling back into the golden glow, and then it began howling even louder as it was burned. When the spirit was hardly larger than a hamster, I took my chance. I dove forward and placed the mason jar beside it, and it was sucked into the jar. I quickly screwed the lid shut.

"There," I said with a sigh, wiping beads of sweat off my forehead. "We stopped it."

Kelly and David both fell backward in relief. After a

moment, the glow around Kelly's body vanished, and her Nai Nai reappeared at her shoulder once more.

"Be glad I was here," Kelly said, brushing dust off her shoulder. "What would you two have done without me? I pretty much just saved the whole school." Being her humble self, as always.

"With *our* help," David added sourly.

"It's because we worked together that we were able to bring down that spirit," I said. Yes, maybe Kelly and her overspirit had taken on the bulk of the task, but David and I were the ones who'd physically captured the evil spirit. Plus, it had been my idea to lure the spirit into the court-yard in the first place. It was annoying to hear Kelly talk like we'd just stood there doing nothing.

Kelly leaned down to tie her shoelaces, not acknowledg-ing what either of us had said.

The tension between David and Kelly practically caused the air between them to crackle. Oh boy. I could sense that I needed to intervene before these two declared an all-out war.

"You know, we don't make a half-bad team," I said. "We managed to capture those spirits without even using our overspirits' powers. Kelly, if you teamed up with David and me, together we could probably round up all the loose spir-its pretty easily." There. Though it meant swallowing my pride, I knew the right thing to do—for Groton's sake—was to extend this olive branch of comradery to Kelly. After all, the Spirit Council had sent her here to work *with* us, not separate from us. And I wasn't so proud that I couldn't admit to recognizing a capable shaman when I spotted one.

Kelly lifted her head, and her sharp gaze met mine. She tilted her head to the side and bit her lip, as though seriously considering my offer. I waited with bated breath. Kelly wasn't exactly friends with David and me, but maybe she would recognize what I already had—that we were stronger when we teamed up.

And, if I was honest with myself, I was less worried about my own shortcomings as a new shaman when there was a more advanced shaman like Kelly around. The most important task at hand was protecting Groton from evil, after all. If that meant setting aside my pride and working together with less-than-pleasant but talented shamans, then so be it.

"Nah," Kelly said after a long moment passed.

My insides deflated with disappointment. I'd half expected that response, but it still stung to be shot down like that. "No?"

"No." Kelly got up and brushed dirt off her pants, then swung her hair over her shoulder. She snapped her fingers, and the spirit of her grandmother vanished into thin air. Despite myself, I couldn't help but think that was cool, and wonder when I'd be advanced enough to summon and dismiss my overspirit at will. "I'm good. I'm a one-girl team, and you two probably couldn't keep up with me."

"Are you kidding me? We so could. We just did!" David

stood up quickly, glaring at Kelly's back. "Whatever. Winnie and I didn't even want to work with you in the first place! Who wants to team up with a know-it-all?"

"David, don't say that," I hissed.

He whirled around, now turning his glare on to me. "What? Kelly is *insufferable*. We could never team up with her. She won't even be in Groton for long anyway, because YOU AND I ARE TOTALLY GOING TO CAPTURE ALL THE SPIRITS AROUND HERE WITHOUT ANY UNWANTED HELP FROM RUDE PEOPLE!" He hollered the last part, but it didn't seem like Kelly had heard. She had already disappeared back inside the building.

"Ow," I winced. "You yelled in my ear."

"Oh. Sorry."

I sighed. There was no question that it had been a team effort to capture these spirits—a task that none of us could have handled on our own. But with David and Kelly at each other's throats like this, it was going to take a miracle to get them to cooperate again.

Well, let the record show that I'd at least tried to keep the peace.

CHAPTER FOURTEEN

"Three shamans to take down **one** measly class two spirit? Are you trying to make me laugh?" My grandmother paced back and forth on the carpet in my room, pausing only to glare at me. Well, she wasn't *on* the carpet, exactly; she hovered half an inch above it. It was the evening already, and Chinese school had ended hours ago.

It had been a strange day, to say the least. After my Chinese school had almost been attacked by a spirit—for a second time, since the first time was at the Mid-Autumn Festival—I'd managed to have another normal hour of class, even though I'd been shaken. On the drive home from Chinese school, I'd asked Lisa why she'd asked me to meet her in the courtyard when she wasn't even there, and she'd been totally confused, even after I'd shown her the texts that *she* had sent. That had ticked me off. There was no way Lisa didn't remember sending those messages. But at least she was safe from the spirits' attack—for now.

"Well? Are you trying to make me laugh?" my grandmother repeated, sounding more cross than ever. Her sharp voice brought me back to the present.

"I'm not trying to make you laugh, Lao Lao," I grumbled. "I didn't bring any almond cookies or anything to help fight spirits, and you weren't there at Chinese school with me. The spirit disguised itself as our vice principal. Only Kelly had her overspirit. What was I supposed to do?"

That didn't earn me Lao Lao's sympathy at all. "And whose fault is that? I've told you and told you, you need to bring me with you to avoid situations like this."

I glanced over at Jade, who was sleeping peacefully on my bed, completely oblivious to the argument going on around her. "Yeah, well, the day you can totally stay connected to the human world without being near Jade, and I don't have to break a million regulations about animals, I'll start taking you around with me."

"That day may be soon, child."

I blinked. "What? Really?"

Lao Lao stroked her chin and stared off into the distance, as though thinking hard. "I've been in the human world for . . . nearly two months now. All the while, my spirit has been establishing some deep roots in this world— thanks to my connection to *you*, child."

"Roots?" I said. "Like a tree?" As I spoke, the image of my grandmother sprouting roots and branches like a tree was so silly that I let out a giggle, which earned me a frown.

"Yes, a bit like a tree. Eventually, when our connection is strong enough, I'll be able to move around without being anchored to Jade. However, that depends on your development as a shaman. You need to train harder and get better at controlling your powers in order for our connection to strengthen. I have full faith in your abilities, Winnie." Lao Lao winked at me.

If I could take my grandmother around with me to public places without having to hide a whole rabbit, that would solve my biggest problem. "How soon do you think I can reach that level, Lao Lao?"

My grandmother shrugged. "It's hard to say. This is not an exact science, you know. Every shaman is different. As long as you keep focusing on honing your powers, I know you'll get there."

I hated it when adults got vague about important stuff like that. Hopefully nothing too terrible would attack before I could train enough to create such a strong connection with my grandmother. But it was true that *something* terrible was in the air. These spirit attacks were growing more and more frequent, with the spirits able to disguise themselves better among the humans.

This wasn't something I could handle on my own. I didn't want to go to the Spirit Council for help, though. Not yet. I didn't want to bother them with anything less than an emergency. Besides, that one lady—Zhula—had seemed extra skeptical of my abilities. The last thing I wanted was to go back now looking incapable, and prove her right.

The next day, after school, David and I had an emergency meeting at the tree house in his backyard, which he called the Clubhouse of Champions. If we didn't succeed on our latest mission, he was going to have to rename it the Clubhouse of Chumps.

"I called this meeting so we could look at the facts. We don't know who these spirits are that are disguising themselves as humans, and we can't even search for information in the records, because so many disappeared." David was sprawled out on the floor of the tree house, a long piece of white paper next to him. Using a black brush, he was drawing complex calligraphy characters onto the paper. David drew his source of power from his calligraphy, and it seemed that the more complicated the characters were, the more power he earned. As soon as he finished the last character, the piece of paper glowed with a golden light that traveled from David's fingertips into the rest of his body.

"Yeah, that sounds about right. We basically have no clues to go on to track down the culprits," I said grimly. When David put it that way, I realized our situation was even worse than I'd thought.

David heaved a long-suffering sigh. The light had faded, and now he rolled up the paper and tucked it into his back pocket. "Great. So what are we going to do?"

"Well, you should get up off the floor first," said Joe. "It's hardly a sanitary place to be lying!"

I had to agree. The tree house was made of wood, and I

didn't even want to think about what tiny insects might be crawling about. Plus, I was currently in the middle of eating a bag of almond cookies to prepare for training, and the crumbs were getting all over the floor. Whoops.

"You both need to train more," Lao Lao harrumphed.

"Besides training," David amended, getting to his feet. "What can we do besides training? How are we going to protect Groton from spirits we know so little about, especially if they can disguise themselves so well among humans? There haven't been any reports of people behaving oddly in the past few days."

"Isn't that a good thing?" I said.

David shook his head. "No. Of course not. That means the spirits have learned how to blend in better with the humans. For all we know, they could be anyone we bump into on the street."

A shiver ran down my spine at the thought of passing by people who weren't actually people. Following David's words, the mood in the room became noticeably gloomier. When he put it that way, trying to stay on guard against this threat was pretty much impossible.

"Well, Xiao Mao said that the spirits are bound to come out during Halloween," I said, mostly to break the heavy silence. "Halloween is a few days away. That still gives us some time to train and capture spirits. Then, when the rest of the spirits strike on Halloween, we'll take them down, and Groton will be spirit-free once more." I spoke with what I hoped was much more confidence than I felt.

After a pause, David sighed. He muttered something that sounded a lot like "Groton had a nice run."

"We'll train you hard, then," said Lao Lao.

"I'd better not see any slacking from either of you," Joe added.

David and I glanced at each other and nodded. I gulped. Halloween was right around the corner. And before then, I *needed* to master combining with my grandmother's spirit.

"You need to empty your mind, Winnie," Lao Lao scolded. "Look at David. He's very good at that."

I snickered. "That's 'cause his head is always empty."

"Hey!" David had had his eyes closed while he slowed his breathing according to Joe's instructions, but now his eyes flew open. An irritated expression replaced his peaceful one. "What's that supposed to mean?"

"David, focus," Joe snapped. It was rare to see the overspirit this serious about training. Rather than keep arguing, David and I both shut up and resumed our concentration. Today was not the day to mess around.

It was a few hours later, getting close to dinnertime. For most of the afternoon, Joe and Lao Lao had been trying to help David and me meditate into a more calm, focused state of mind. Once we succeeded with that, it would be much easier to combine with our overspirits. Getting to that point, however, seemed next to impossible at the moment, especially with Lao Lao practically breathing down my neck.

"You're still distracted," my grandmother remarked.

"How am I supposed to empty my mind with you swooping around my head like that?" I grumbled. Though I'd eaten all the almond cookies I'd brought with me, my powers were still taking their sweet time warming up.

"I don't care how—just do it!" said my grandmother. But at least she gave me more space, backing away from me.

I gritted my teeth in frustration. It wasn't just Lao Lao distracting me. Thoughts of my schoolwork, of the spirits running around on the loose—all of that was taking up space in my head. How exactly *was* I supposed to empty my mind when there were a million things to be worrying about? How could *anyone?*

Plus, every time I did get close to emptying my mind, that same mental block would emerge, preventing me from fully combining my mind with Lao Lao's.

"Just pretend you're taking a math test," David suggested. "I'm sure your mind will go blank in no time."

"That's not funny," I snapped. David stuck out his tongue at me in response.

"Neither of you is concentrating properly," Lao Lao sighed, shaking her head. Her voice was heavy with weariness.

"I think we should just let the evil spirits take over Groton," Joe said mildly, picking at his fingernail. "They may do a better job of running it than these humans."

My grandmother glared. "Oh, shut it, you."

"Okay, okay," I said, putting my hands up. The way that the two overspirits were glaring at each other told me things were getting way too heated. "I *really* won't be able to keep my mind clear if everyone keeps arguing."

"Good point," Lao Lao said, nodding. "Joe, stop being immature."

"I was not being—"

"Winnie, David, continue!" Lao Lao barked, as though Joe hadn't said anything.

I shut my eyes, doing my best to concentrate again. This time, my insides began to grow warmer, the telltale sign that my powers were working. The familiar warmth filled me up. I pushed against the mental block, using all my focus. After a minute of intense concentration, I finally broke through it. And then I heard Lao Lao's voice again, but this time in my head.

Winnie, can you hear me?

Yes, I answered.

The connection wasn't very strong, and it was much more taxing than I remembered—it was taking all my focus and energy to maintain this fragile telepathic communication with my grandmother. But it was still more progress than I'd made in weeks.

I did it, I thought. *We did it, Lao Lao!*

As soon as that thought passed through my mind, just like that, the connection was severed. One moment, there was a warmth filling my insides. The next thing I knew, I could no longer hear Lao Lao's voice in my head or sense her presence. As fast as it had come, the connection had disappeared. Guess I'd celebrated getting over the mental block too soon.

I opened my eyes. My grandmother hovered above, shaking her head slightly as though to reorient herself.

"Well," said Lao Lao, "that was a start."

But even if she didn't say it in so many words, I could hear the disappointment in her voice. I still had a long way to go before mastering combining, and we were running out of time fast. That brief combination had drained me of almost all my energy.

"I—I keep getting a mental block when I try to combine," I blurted, looking around at Lao Lao, David, and Joe. "Has that ever happened to you?"

Judging by the clueless expressions on their faces, I was alone in this.

"A mental block?" Lao Lao asked, shaking her head. "No, I can't say that's happened to me before."

"Perhaps you're trying too hard to force a connection," Joe said. "Psyching yourself out."

I looked at David, but he just shrugged. "Yeah, never happened to me."

Of course not. Now I wished I'd kept my struggles to myself. My cheeks flamed. The others probably thought I wasn't that great a shaman, if I was experiencing these strange mental blocks. Bet Kelly had never experienced

these blocks, either. My goal of becoming the best shaman possible was slipping further and further away. It was
enough to make anyone frustrated.

"Are you feeling okay, Winnie?" My grandmother peered
at me in concern.

"Today's shamans are so fragile," Joe said in a carrying
whisper. "Headaches at the slightest strain."

"I don't have a headache," I snapped, glowering at him.
Joe just glanced down and picked at his cuticles. "And I am
not *fragile*."

"Never mind," said David, for once not taking the opportunity to brag, even though he'd just successfully combined with Joe. That was how I knew the situation was
getting really dire. "Let's take a break and brainstorm a plan
of attack for Halloween."

Doing my best not to think about how behind I was in
my training, I nodded. It was time to come up with a con-
crete battle plan.

"David! Are you up there?" A woman's voice floated up
toward us from the ground.

"That's my mom. She must be back early from her book
club meeting," David murmured, more to himself than to
me. He leaned his head out the window and shouted, "Yeah,
I'm up here with Winnie!"

"What are you doing?"

"Um . . . m-math problems," David lied.

"Oh, I love Winnie. Well, come down here, kids!" Mrs.
Zuo shouted. "I brought snacks for you."

I didn't know much about David's mom, aside from the fact that she was a stay-at-home mom and that she was really good at Chinese card games. (Every time my parents invited the Zuos over to our house, they'd complain later about how Mrs. Zuo had creamed them once again.)

"Weird," David said. "My mom's acting weird."

"It's weird for her to feed you snacks?"

"No, I mean, she doesn't even like you."

I frowned. "Wow. Thank you." But now that David mentioned that, I *did* recall that Mrs. Zuo had thought I was a bad influence on David, just because once when we were seven, I dared him to draw mustaches on the Zuos' kitchen place mats. I was pretty sure Mrs. Zuo had never forgiven me for that stunt, which was a bit long to hold a grudge, if you ask me. I mean, we were *seven*.

When we climbed down from the Clubhouse of Champions, Mrs. Zuo was beaming at us, holding bags of shrimp chips in her hands. She hugged David, which caused him to give her a strange look. Come to think of it, I'd never seen David's parents hug him before.

"Um . . . Mom? You good?" David asked once she'd let him go. He'd frozen in shock.

"Never been better," said Mrs. Zuo cheerily. She handed a bag of chips to each of us. "Here. Extra energy to tackle your math problems."

"But you never let me have shrimp chips," David said, gawking at his bag as though he'd never seen something like it before. "You say fried foods are bad for my skin."

"Did I say that?" Mrs. Zuo's brows furrowed as she seemed to consider this. "Well, I've had a change of heart."

"Hey, if you don't want your shrimp chips, I'll take them." I held out my free hand toward David.

"Yeah, right!" He popped open his bag of chips and shoved a few into his mouth. "Thanks, Mom. Winnie, let's get back to work."

We left Mrs. Zuo smiling and waving at us. As I climbed back up the tree house, I glanced back. For a moment I thought she was glaring, but when I did a double take, that smile was back on her face.

CHAPTER FIFTEEN

Mama surprised me later that day by coming home early from teaching class. These days, she'd been staying after, and like Baba she was pretty exhausted by the time she got home. Honestly, I never want to grow up. I know a lot of kids who can't wait to be older, but I don't see the appeal of it at all. Being an adult looks so tiring.

When I was in the middle of finishing up my history homework, Mama poked her head into my room. "Winnie? Are you busy?"

I closed my textbook and turned around. "No, why?"

"One of my coworkers suggested I try making this egg-tart recipe," Mama said, holding up a piece of paper in her hand. "I know I've been busy, and we haven't had much time together lately. Would you like to make these egg tarts with me?"

My face broke out into a grin, and I practically leapt off my bed. "Yeah!" As if I would ever turn down the chance to bake and eat something yummy, especially egg tarts. If you haven't had egg tarts before, you're seriously missing out.

Mama had already gotten the ingredients out onto the

kitchen island, so all that was left to do was follow the instructions on the recipe. Though we hadn't had time to bake together in weeks, we soon fell into a comfortable rhythm. I sifted together flour, salt, and sugar in a mixing bowl to make the dough, while Mama worked on creating the custard filling by dissolving salt and sugar into hot water.

"Is there something bothering you, Winnie?" my mother asked as I was beating the egg yolks. "I sense that something is weighing heavily on your mind."

For a moment I considered brushing off Mama's concern and pretending I was completely fine, but then I decided against it. Mama had a sixth sense for figuring out when Lisa and I were feeling down in the dumps.

"Um . . ." I had to rack my brain, trying to figure out what bits of the truth I could tell Mama without revealing the huge secret I was keeping—being a shaman and, you know, saving the world. Not only was I required to keep that under wraps, but even if I *did* let my mother in on that bit of knowledge, she'd think I was pulling her leg. "Oh . . . um . . . I've just been . . . stressed lately," I said.

"About what? School?" Mama motioned for me to hand the dough to her, and I obeyed, then watched her slice it into equal parts.

"Um, yeah, school." I nodded enthusiastically, grateful for the plausible explanation. Actually, school hadn't been on my mind all that much lately. I'd been preoccupied with training as much as I could with Halloween approaching, doing my best to live up to the Spirit Council's expectations, and keeping the peace between David and Kelly. . . .

Kelly! Now *there* was a tidbit of truth I could tell Mama. "Oh, and there's a new girl in my class—Kelly. Kelly Miao."

"Miao?" Mama paused in the middle of slicing and stared off into the distance, squinting in concentration. "That's a Chinese name, isn't it?"

I nodded.

"Strange. That surname doesn't ring a bell. I don't know any Miaos who live around here."

My mother prided herself on being in contact with all the Chinese families in Groton, especially because there weren't that many. "Well, like I said, Kelly just moved here," I said. "You'll probably meet her parents at some point later."

"Hmm. I see. Is Kelly nice?" Mama sprayed the tart pan with oil and then handed over a few pieces of dough. "Here. Roll them into balls and put them into the molds."

I followed Mama's instructions, wondering what I should tell her about Kelly. Nice? I wouldn't have called her *nice*. On the spectrum of nice to mean, Kelly was definitely closer to mean. But even though her words often came across as cold, somehow I didn't think she meant to be mean.

"Well, Kelly is . . . she . . . she's smart and talented," I finally said. Maybe it was best to just be truthful. It wasn't like my words would get back to Kelly, anyway. All the words I'd been dying to say burst forth. "She's making David and me look bad in school. And she's also better than us at, um . . ."

I tried to think of a stand-in phrase for *shaman training,* since obviously I couldn't tell Mama about that. "*Extracurriculars.* David doesn't like her, either."

"Really? David is so nice to everyone, though."

I resisted the urge to roll my eyes all the way up to the ceiling. Mama only thought David was nice because David was a suck-up to all the aunties and uncles, putting on the front of being the perfect kid. He had everyone fooled. As sharp as she was, my mother could also be pretty oblivious at times.

"Well, Kelly hasn't been that nice to David, either. If you ask me, Kelly's a little too cocky. Like, yeah, she's smart and everything, but does she have to go around parading it?" I accidentally pressed down too hard on a piece of dough, squashing it flat instead of rolling it into a ball. Oops.

I knew I should've kept my big mouth shut the moment when Mama turned toward me with a stern frown. Though that didn't have quite the effect she intended, given how her face had smudges of dough on it. "Well, Winnie, it sounds to me like you're envious of Kelly."

"I'm not envious of—" Okay, there was no point in denying something so obvious. "Maybe a little."

"Try not to let that feeling get to you. There's always going to be someone better than you. There are billions of people on the planet. There are thousands, *millions,* better than you."

If Mama meant to make me feel better, she was doing a real bang-up job of it. Imagining millions of Kellys running around this planet made me want to get *off* the planet. "Gee, thanks."

"I'm saying this to help you put the situation into perspective, Winnie," Mama said wisely. We'd finished filling the tart molds with dough, and now Mama was pouring the custard inside them. "Rather than viewing this new girl as competition, you could learn from her."

"*Learn* from her?" I spluttered. As if. The idea of going up to Kelly and asking if I could learn from her was about as appealing as eating rocks. I could just picture the pompous look on Kelly's face if David and I went to her for advice on leveling up as shamans. She'd probably laugh herself silly. Then she'd refuse to help us. "Never. Not in this lifetime." I stubbornly crossed my arms over my chest as I watched Mama put the tray into the oven.

When she'd closed the oven door, Mama straightened and turned toward me. "You could try to work together with Kelly. I'm sure she has weaknesses where you have strengths."

Kelly? Weaknesses? Not likely. "I already offered to do something like that," I muttered, remembering how at Chinese school, Kelly had shot down my proposal to work together to capture the rogue spirits. "I wanted Kelly to team up with David and me for a, um . . . a special project. She didn't even consider it."

"Well, then, she must not be that smart after all," Mama said matter-of-factly.

Dang. If Kelly had heard what my mother had just said,

she would've been real mad. But Mama was kind of right, wasn't she? Even though I hated to admit it, I knew that Kelly, David, and I—and therefore Groton—would be better off if we worked together rather than letting our pride get in the way. The fact that Kelly didn't understand that was not only frustrating, but also showed that she wasn't quite as brilliant as she clearly thought she was.

"You should still do your best not to butt heads with her," my mother added, as though she could hear my thoughts. "Maybe you and David can start up a nice conversation with Kelly next time you see her. Try to see eye to eye with each other."

I could think of a million things I'd rather do than make nice with Kelly when *she* was the one being insufferable, but I decided to keep that to myself. Besides, maybe it was because of the aroma of egg tarts filling the air, but I was feeling less annoyed than before. "I guess," I said. Maybe I'd try one more time to get Kelly and David to see my point of view. Kelly wasn't the only concern weighing on my mind, though. "Um . . . and there's one more thing, Mama."

"Yes?"

"So the last few weeks, I've been . . . studying . . . really hard, because I have this upcoming . . . test." Of course, Mama didn't know that by *studying* I actually meant *training,* and that by *test* I actually meant *impossibly stressful task to capture rogue spirits and protect Groton.* "And this test is going to be really, *really* hard. I'm scared that I'll fail, even after all my studying." The words rushed out of my mouth, and instantly I felt a bit of relief. I hadn't realized that holding in my worries had been burdening me so much until this moment.

Mama studied me, her expression unreadable. "Well, Winnie, you don't need me to tell you that you're a smart girl, and that you're probably being silly and will do just fine on this test. But it's natural to feel fear when you're facing a challenge, even if you've spent a long time preparing for it," she said wisely. "Do you want to know a secret? I get scared when I have to teach a new class."

"You *do?*" I gasped. Mama taught college for a living, and I'd sat in on her classes once for Take Your Child to Work Day. She hadn't seemed to have any kind of fear of public speaking.

"Yes, of course. It's only natural to feel nervous when you're facing the unknown. In fact, before I became a teacher, public speaking was my greatest fear. I had to go against my natural instincts to conquer my fear. And I'm very glad I did, because I love teaching."

Wow. My mother was much braver than I'd known. She probably would have made a great shaman—maybe better than me, if the power hadn't skipped her generation. "How did you make yourself get over your fear?"

"The trick is not to dwell so much on your fear that you end up self-sabotaging. There's no use worrying about everything that could go wrong, when you could be focusing that energy on making sure that you put your best foot forward."

Mama's words made so much sense. Maybe the reason I'd been experiencing that mental block during training was because I was blocking *myself* from combining with Lao Lao, all because of my own doubts. If I didn't believe in my own ability to take down these rogue spirits, then how could I possibly succeed when the moment of truth arrived?

The timer on Mama's phone went off, interrupting my thoughts. "Oh, the egg tarts are ready!" I shouted, pointing toward the oven.

Mama grabbed the oven mitts and yanked open the oven door, causing hot air to waft toward us. After carefully taking out the piping-hot tray, she used a toothpick to poke the egg tarts in their middle. Mama made sure to never let me handle the oven when she was around. "They're done," she announced when she was satisfied with poking the egg tarts. "We'll wait at least ten minutes for these egg tarts to cool before we try them. In the meantime—why don't you practice piano for me, Winnie? I don't believe you've practiced yet this afternoon."

I sighed. Mama was right, of course. "Fine."

I trudged into the living room and managed to bumble my way through Bach's Concerto in D Minor a couple of times by the time Mama called me back into the kitchen to try the egg tarts. Mine was still pretty hot when I bit into it, but I didn't mind, because it was fluffy and light and *delicious*. Like its own kind of magic.

"How is it?" Mama asked.

"Perfect," I said through a mouth full of egg tart.

"Good." My mother and I shared a smile.

Maybe it was just the delicious food putting me in an agreeable mood, but in that moment, I made up my mind. For the good of Groton, I was going to do my best to believe in my own shaman abilities. And, whether David and Kelly liked it or not, I was going to give this shaman teamwork thing one more shot.

CHAPTER SIXTEEN

"Kelly, you got a moment?"

I stopped by Kelly's locker as the sixth graders headed toward the cafeteria for lunch. Her expression was unreadable, as always. I could never tell if she was in a good mood or a bad one, because I hadn't yet seen that expression change.

"Um, yeah, sure." Kelly gave me a distracted look. "What is it?"

I took a deep breath. This probably wasn't going to go well, but I'd still rather give it another shot than give up. "Well, you remember the other day at Chinese school, how I said that you and David and I should team up?"

Kelly rolled her eyes. "Oh, not this again."

Not this again? With Kelly's rude words, all goodwill left my body. Mama had been wrong, and now I felt like an idiot to have come up to Kelly just to have my idea rejected again. I wasn't going to try to make nice with Kelly if she wouldn't even meet me in the middle. Seriously, what was her problem? Just because she had a little more experience than David and me didn't make her somehow better than us or out of our league. At the end of the day, we were all shamans, and we all had the same goal—to protect Groton.

I forced myself to swallow those words, at least for now. She wasn't more likely to work with me if I was yelling at her.

"Listen, I'm just trying to look out for the town," I said in as patient a tone as I could manage. "I know you think you're better off working on your own, but three of us together could really—"

"In case you haven't noticed, since I arrived—and especially in the last couple of days—there have been much fewer spirit attacks," Kelly interrupted. "Why do you think that is? It's because I'm capable of handling the spirits on my own. They know it, and they're frightened to come out now."

I wanted to argue, but found that technically Kelly wasn't wrong. Though I'd been expecting tons more spirit activity now that we were so close to Halloween, not much had happened recently. But my gut still told me something was off. It was almost . . . eerie, that nothing had gone wrong lately. I didn't think this was due to Kelly's presence, but I didn't have any evidence to prove the contrary, either. What if this peace was due to evil spirits regrouping to plan something big?

"If you really want to look out for the town, then you'd better stop trying to change my mind, and prepare yourself. Something's going to happen on Halloween, in two days," Kelly said bluntly. Her tone wasn't mean, but rather sounded like a warning. "Things are going to get very, very heated around here. And I'm not just talking about the costume contest."

"Yeah, of course I know," I said. "I've known for a little while now."

"You and David don't have to worry about a thing, though," she continued, patting me on the shoulder in a condescending way. "Just carry on as usual. I'm more than capable of handling all the spirits on my own. In fact, I prefer it. You rookie agents would just get in the way."

Knowing Kelly, she already had a fourteen-point attack plan to capture all the spirits. And she'd execute it flawlessly, too. She practically oozed confidence right now.

I took a deep breath, trying to calm my suddenly racing pulse. Why couldn't Kelly go just one day without being a constant thorn in my side? Even if she didn't want to work together with David and me, that didn't mean she had to throw her superiority into my face. I was sick of her taking every opportunity to lord it over us.

Sorry, Mama, but you were mistaken to think that talking to Kelly again would sway her. She really is just a cocky jerk.

I drew myself up to my full height and looked Kelly square in the eye. Even though I didn't feel confident, I had to fake it. I had to pretend to be every bit as confident as Kelly seemed to be. "No way. We'll be the ones to protect this town from evil," I blustered. David and I were a *we* now. I didn't know how to feel about that. The enemy of my enemy really *was* my friend, I guessed.

Kelly scoffed and rolled her eyes. "I didn't say that to argue with you, Winnie. I just told you the facts so you know what to expect. Anyway, I'll see you at lunch." And before I could get a word in edgewise, Kelly flounced off down the hall.

My fingers clenched around my lunch-box handle. David and I were going to successfully protect Groton without Kelly's help. And we were going to make her eat her words, no matter what.

Though Halloween was normally one of my favorite days of the year, this year I was barely able to get into the spirit. (No pun intended.) It was hard to get excited about dressing up and trick-or-treating and eating candy when the constant threat of danger loomed over my head. While everyone else was having fun planning to dress up as fake evil creatures, I had to worry about *real* evil creatures. In the hallway after lunch, I overheard Tracy complaining to Jessamyn that she still couldn't choose which costume she was going to wear to school on Halloween. I would've given anything for my outfit to be my biggest problem.

The day before Halloween, it was time to get to work. I needed to make as many almond cookies as possible—some for Mrs. Payton's class party, and some for spirit-battling purposes. The ones for the party definitely wouldn't be magical. After I got home from school, I rushed around the kitchen gathering all the ingredients and appliances I needed. Normally, baking something yummy would be the highlight of my day. But even baking cookies had lost its appeal. I really preferred baking cookies for fun, not because the fate of the world possibly depended on me making a really powerful batch of magical almond cookies.

"Winnie, are you even paying attention?"

Oh, crap. The flour spilled out of the measuring cup and onto the surface of the kitchen island. I'd been so consumed by my own thoughts that I hadn't paid any mind to what I was doing.

Lao Lao floated nearby, a scowl on her face. She crossed her arms over her chest. "Your head is in the clouds. You're not focused at all. You didn't even measure out the correct amount of flour."

I stared down at the gloopy mess in the mixing bowl. Oops. My grandmother was right. I'd meant to double the recipe, adding two and two-thirds cups of flour to the eggs in the bowl, but I'd only added one and one-third. Also, a bunch of it had spilled onto the counter. *Rookie,* I could hear Kelly saying.

"I'll start over," I sighed.

"I think you should go get your head straight first," Lao Lao said sternly. I opened my mouth to argue that my head *was* on straight, but my grandmother raised a hand and narrowed her eyes at me, and I faltered. Her lips pressed into a thin line. "There's no way I can let you use an oven the way you are right now. It would be dangerous."

"But, Lao Lao—"

"No buts," my grandmother interjected. She crossed her arms over her chest and opened her mouth to say something, but before she could, she was interrupted by the sound of footsteps heading toward the kitchen.

"Winnie," came Lisa's voice.

It took every ounce of self-control not to roll my eyes. What did Lisa want now? "What?"

My sister poked her head into the kitchen. Of course, she couldn't see my grandmother's spirit, so her glare was fixed on me—and the mess of ingredients in the kitchen. I braced myself for her to make a comment about me baking, but instead she just said, "It's about time to practice piano today, isn't it, Winnie?"

"You sound like Mama," I groaned.

Instead of firing back like she normally would, Lisa blinked, a look of surprise on her face. "Do I really? Oops." She muttered something else to herself that I didn't quite catch.

I stared, and then shook my head. Whatever. I didn't have any time to wonder about Lisa's odd behavior. Lao Lao was nodding in approval at Lisa's suggestion, and I *had* really been slacking on piano practice lately. Even though I'd still been practicing at least an hour every day, it was half-hearted practice at best. Mrs. Kotova hadn't scheduled me for any competitions or recitals this fall, but if I didn't want to be totally terrible at the annual test this winter, then I'd have to get serious about piano again soon.

My life was basically on fire, and Groton was in danger from the oncoming spirit attack on Halloween, but I still couldn't fall behind on piano.

The one good thing I could say about piano was that it was calming. Even if I had to be dragged kicking and screaming to the piano bench, whenever I finished a practice session, I'd always feel a lot more settled down. Not to mention, I'd be ready to fall asleep—sometimes right at the piano bench. Perfect pre-bedtime activity.

I returned to the kitchen after pounding out Beethoven's Bagatelle in G Minor a few times, suppressing a yawn. My grandmother gave me an approving nod, which I took as a sign that I could go ahead and make all the cookies I needed to—properly this time.

I started out with the almond cookies I needed for my power. This time, I was careful to measure out exactly double of each ingredient, and to follow the instructions in Lao Lao's cookbook to a T. I used about half the dough, setting aside the rest for later.

"You're not going to bake all of it?" Lao Lao asked.

I shook my head. "Not yet."

Soon the kitchen filled with the smell of cookies as they baked in the oven. My mouth watered. I could practically taste the warm, delectable cookies already and feel the way they'd melt on my tongue.

When the almond cookies were done baking, I set them aside to cool. Then it was time to bake cookies for my class's Halloween party.

"Why don't you just give them almond cookies?" Lao Lao said.

"I wanna try something else."

My grandmother gave me a curious look, but she didn't press. I rummaged through the cabinet next to the refrigerator, until I found what I was looking for, right between the bag of sugar and the cinnamon jar—semisweet chocolate chips.

I opened the bag of chocolate chips and dumped them into the remainder of the almond cookie dough. Then I stirred them in. This wasn't my first time modifying a recipe, but it was definitely my first time modifying one of my grandmother's.

"What are you doing, Winnie?" Lao Lao didn't sound upset, just confused. "These cookies won't contain any magic inside them. They won't be useful to you tomorrow."

"I know. I won't be the one eating them. They're for my class Halloween party."

"Oh."

Silence fell between my grandmother and me as I kneaded the chocolate-chip-almond cookie dough, breaking it down into twenty even chunks. I placed the cookies onto the parchment paper on top of a tray. Then, while wearing oven mitts, I put them carefully into the oven.

"Why use chocolate?" Lao Lao asked.

I shrugged. "Everyone loves chocolate chip cookies." I'd never met someone who didn't like chocolate chip cookies. I was beginning to think people like that didn't exist.

When the oven timer dinged, I carefully took the piping-hot cookies out of the oven and placed them beside the regular almond cookies. Then I glanced up at the clock. It was only four o'clock. Mama wouldn't be home for another two hours, and Baba would come home past dinnertime. There was plenty of time to let these cookies cool and pack them up for the next day.

With this, I was fully prepared to face whatever happened tomorrow on Halloween. The class party, the spirit attack . . .

Come at me, world. Winnie Zeng isn't scared of anything.

Out of nowhere came the sound of a phone vibrating on the dining table, shattering the quiet of the house. "AHHHHHHH!" I screamed, nearly jumping out of my skin.

Lao Lao sighed and shook her head at me, muttering something that sounded an awful lot like "The world is doomed."

Okay, so starting *now*, I wouldn't be scared of anything.

The phone wouldn't stop vibrating. Was it mine? No, mine was in my pocket. I moved over to the table. Weird. It was Baba's phone. I recognized it quickly because his was the only one with a black OtterBox case. Why wouldn't my father have his phone on him at work, though? Had he forgotten it this morning?

After a second, the phone stopped vibrating. I picked

it up and saw a green missed-call notification flash across the screen. It was from BOSS. Oh boy. Was Baba in trouble because he hadn't brought his phone to work or something?

The phone began buzzing with another incoming call, from BOSS again.

"Can't you make that noise stop?" Lao Lao complained, glowering at the phone as though it had personally offended her.

"Not unless I turn off the phone," I replied.

"Well, then, turn it off!"

I guess Baba wouldn't be able to access this phone anyway while he was at work, so there was no point in leaving it on. I turned it off, and the calls stopped. Hopefully Baba wouldn't get in trouble for not bringing his cell phone to work. Besides, if he was in the office, why wouldn't his boss just go talk to him in person?

Whatever. Adults were weird, and the stuff they did often didn't make any sense. But still, a tiny part of me sensed that something wasn't quite right—especially because things were too *quiet* now. No spirits had been appearing, though it was the night before Halloween.

It reminded me of the calm before a storm.

CHAPTER SEVENTEEN

Everything started going downhill when I got my tail caught in the bathroom door the next morning.

Not a *real* tail, of course. The short, fluffy black tail that was part of my cat costume. Lisa had taken so long in the bathroom that I'd been in a rush and slammed the bathroom door on the tail. That was annoying, though not the worst thing that could happen, so I tried to forget about it as I brushed my teeth and hair.

The *real* problem was when I went downstairs and found Lisa packing up the chocolate chip almond cookies I'd baked yesterday.

I rushed over. "Hey! What do you think you're doing?"

She shot me an annoyed look. Lisa hadn't dressed up for Halloween at all. I guess high schoolers think they're too cool for that. She didn't need to dress up, though, if you asked me. That glare already made her plenty terrifying. All Lisa needed was a tall, pointy black hat, and she'd make a scary witch.

"I'm taking these cookies for the Key Club fundraiser." Lisa spoke as though explaining something very simple.

"But those are my—" Then my stomach plummeted as the realization struck me. My heart thudded to a stop. Oh no. With everything that had been going on, I'd forgotten that I'd promised to bake cookies for Lisa's Key Club fundraiser.

Her eyes widened, and for a moment I thought they flashed red. But it must've been a trick of the light, because they were dark brown when I looked again. "You . . . did make these for the fundraiser, right?"

I shook my head, my stomach sinking with guilt. "No. Those are for my class Halloween party."

"You forgot." My sister's voice was flat. She didn't sound angry, but that was when Lisa was at her scariest. "Well, that's just great."

That's just great in Lisa-speak meant *I'm going to beat you up.*

It would have been smart of me to back away and leave for school right then and there, but I wasn't in a particularly charitable mood this morning. I wasn't scared of Lisa. In fact, I was getting really annoyed. I was her little sister, yet somehow it seemed that Lisa was the one coming to me for favors instead of the other way around. Why was I the one carrying the responsibility of saving the world on my shoulders *and* baking cookies for Lisa's class?

"What the heck am I supposed to tell the Key Club now?" Lisa snapped, glowering at me.

"Figure it out," I retorted. "That's not my problem."

She reeled as though I'd slapped her. "Ex*cuse* me?"

"Do you need me to repeat myself? You messing up for your fundraiser isn't my problem."

"You promised you'd bake cookies for me," Lisa growled. She was turning redder and redder in the face, and she made an intimidating picture as she towered over me with anger.

I stepped back without thinking, though I wanted to stand my ground. "It's not even my fundraiser, and besides, I'm younger than you! Why couldn't you bake them yourself?"

"I've been super busy."

"So have I."

"I'm no good at baking!"

"You didn't even try!"

"I was counting on you, and I *needed* those cookies, Winnie." Lisa's eyes turned red again, and this time when I blinked, they stayed that way. Whoa. Something was *definitely* wrong here. Was my sister wearing color-changing contacts or something?

"Your eyes—they turned red just now," I gasped.

Lisa glanced in the mirror, then back at me. Her eyes had turned to their normal color. "What? No, they didn't."

"Yes, they did! I know what I saw."

"Do you even hear yourself? Do you know how you sound? How could my eyes change color just like that?" Lisa shook her head.

Even if it didn't make sense, I still knew what I'd seen. I didn't think it had been just a trick of the light. Though now that Lisa's eyes had resumed their usual dark brown, it was harder to remain firm in my stance.

"And don't change the subject, you stupid, foolish little girl," Lisa continued before I could get a word in edgewise. "Those cookies you forgot to make were going to be part of my plan, and now I'll have to come up with another—"

"What is going on this morning?"

Lisa and I stopped glaring at each other at once.

We turned in unison toward the sound of Mama's voice. Mama didn't have to teach any morning classes today, which was why she hadn't been up—well, until now. She frowned from the doorway, crossing her arms over her chest. She was still in her pink bathrobe. "Are you two fighting over cookies?"

"Winnie broke a promise to me," Lisa blurted out.

"Winnie, is that true?" Mama said, turning on me.

Wow. No way was I going to let Lisa twist the situation like that. "Yeah, well, you shouldn't be asking your little sister to promise to make cookies for *your* fundraiser," I fired back. "That's your responsibility, not mine."

Lisa opened her mouth to retort, but Mama cut her off.

"I've heard enough. Winnie, you shouldn't break promises. And, Lisa, you shouldn't be asking Winnie to do your work for you."

I turned my gaze toward the floor so that Mama couldn't see how angry I was. Lisa said nothing, but I knew she had to still be mad, too.

"Winnie, take your cookies to class. Lisa, I'll drive you to the store to pick up something quick."

"Fine," Lisa muttered. But I could tell by her sullen expression that this wasn't over. Well, it wasn't over for me, either. Yeah, maybe I *had* agreed to make cookies for Lisa's fundraiser—but it was totally unfair for her to push her responsibility onto me, and not even bother to help.

"You're taking the bus today, right?" Mama said, eyeing the tray of cookies.

"Yeah," I sighed. I really didn't like taking the smelly old bus, but I couldn't bike while carrying all these cookies.

"Don't be late, Winnie."

"I won't."

Mama moved toward the garage door, but then paused and turned back to me. "By the way, did you hear your father come back home late last night?"

I blinked in surprise at the sudden change in topic. "Um . . . no." I would have definitely heard the garage door open and close, too, because I'd struggled to sleep all night. Hey, you try getting a good night's rest when you know you have to fight evil the next day. My gaze turned toward the dining table, where I'd left Baba's phone yesterday. He must have come home late last night and picked it up, because it was no longer there.

"Strange." Mama's face scrunched up. "He must have been out really late last night. He seems very absent-minded lately."

So I wasn't the only one who'd noticed that Baba's behavior had been a little off.

"I'll text him when I'm at work. Don't be late for school, Winnie, okay?" my mother added distractedly.

"You already said that," I pointed out, but I didn't think my mother even heard me.

And with that, Mama and Lisa left the kitchen to head for the garage. I listened to the sounds of the garage door opening, and then the car engine starting up. Taking deep breaths, I felt my heartbeat slowly begin to settle down again, until I was more annoyed than angered. Then, after a minute, my mother and sister were gone. I glanced up at the clock. It was already seven-fifteen. That gave me only fifteen more minutes until the bus arrived.

Leaving the cookies on the counter, I ran up the stairs to fetch my backpack, as well as Jade—and Lao Lao. Though I really didn't like the idea of bringing my pet rabbit to school and hiding her all day—one more thing to worry about—the idea of being separated from my overspirit today, on Halloween, was much worse. Today of all days, Lao Lao and I needed to be together. Even if that meant risking being caught bringing a rabbit to school.

My grandmother greeted me with a grim expression on her face. It was the face of somebody who knew there was dirty work ahead. But then, as she looked me up and down, the serious look turned into confusion.

"You are planning to fight spirits . . . dressed like that?"

my grandmother said dubiously, staring at my cat costume as though I were wearing a garbage bag. "Do you really think that's practical, Winnie?"

"Well, I can't *not* dress up today," I said. "It's Halloween! Also, I need to dress up if I want to get candy."

At that, Lao Lao gave me a perplexed look. "I don't understand these American customs," she muttered.

I guessed that when my grandmother was growing up in China, there was no such thing as putting on costumes to get free candy from strangers. That was sad to think about.

"Okay. Let's go to your school," my grandmother said. Then she added under her breath, "I sure hope these spirits are scared of cats."

"Just remember the rules."

"Rules?" Lao Lao's expression fell.

"You can't talk to me while I'm in class. Not unless it's an emergency—like, if spirits are attacking." I stared my grandmother straight in the eye so she knew how serious I was. "Unless it's an emergency, even if you do talk to me, I'll ignore you. Got it?"

Lao Lao agreed, though she didn't look happy about it. Then we were off to school, a strange trio of a rabbit, an overspirit, and a girl dressed up as a cat.

Honestly, if I were an evil spirit, I wouldn't even *think* about messing with us.

When I arrived at Mrs. Payton's homeroom that morning, I found the place decked out in even *more* Halloween decorations. Paper ghosts were taped up along the whiteboard. Cobwebs hung from the corners of the room, and our teacher had even strung up black paper bats in addition to the black and orange streamers, which dangled from the ceiling. Mrs. Payton had dressed up as a witch, wearing a black hat and a black-and-purple robe, carrying a broomstick in one hand. She was so into the costume that she'd even painted her skin green.

Almost all my classmates had dressed up for the Halloween party—everyone except Jessamyn, Tracy, and Kim. They were wearing regular clothes—well, regular for them, which was still nice. Jessamyn was wearing a red cardigan, Tracy sported a black jean jacket, and Kim wore a pink sundress. They looked like they were on their way to a photo shoot, which normally would have earned them admiring glances from our classmates. Today, though, people were giggling and giving them weird looks.

"It's so childish to dress up for Halloween," I heard Jessamyn say to Kim in a loud, carrying voice.

But nobody else seemed to care that Jessamyn thought we were "childish." The popular girls were the ones who were awkwardly standing out for once, because everyone else was wearing costumes.

"I told you we should've dressed up," hissed Tracy. Jessamyn turned bright red, and for once, she didn't seem to have a response.

I tried to hide a smile. I must not have done a good job of it, because Kim snapped at me, "What are you looking at?"

"Um . . . n-nothing," I said, hurrying away.

"Psst. Winnie. *Winnie.*" Lao Lao's voice, floating from behind me, sounded urgent.

"What is it?" I whispered out of the corner of my lip, annoyed. "I told you not to talk to me unless it's an emergency."

"I sense some unfriendly presence following us."

"Can you be more specific? Unfriendly like an evil spirit? Or unfriendly like Jessamyn and her friends?" I must have spoken too loudly, because nearby, Melissa gave me a weird look. I flashed her a tight smile, and she quickly moved across the room. Whoops.

"I can't pinpoint what this presence is specifically," my grandmother said. "That's the worrisome part. Normally my powers are strong enough to identify an unwelcome presence. But this time . . ."

Well, that definitely wasn't the most comforting thing to hear, but it wasn't exactly an emergency. And even when I forced myself to concentrate, I couldn't sense anything supernatural in the vicinity.

"Wow, Winnie, you dressed up as a cat? That's so basic."

An obnoxious voice broke through my focus. I'd have recognized that voice anywhere. Frowning, I turned to see . . . somebody wearing a round gold hat that was too big for his head. It was David. He wore a gold shirt, red pants, and a piece of red fabric tied around his neck. In his left hand he clutched a small red stick that had gold bands on either end. This was one of the most mysterious getups I'd seen in my entire life. It was strange even for David.

"What are you supposed to be?" I blurted out. "Ketchup and mustard?"

"Ketchup and *what*?" David stared at me with his mouth open, looking so affronted you would've thought I'd sworn at him. "Why are you so . . . so . . . *ugh*." He flapped his arms around. He couldn't even finish whatever he was about to say about me. Though it was probably better for my self-esteem if David kept it at that.

"Well, what's with the red-and-yellow theme, then?" I said, annoyed. "What else are people supposed to think of, besides ketchup and mustard?"

Just then, Joe came floating up behind David. I startled. He'd been so quiet for once that I hadn't even noticed his presence here. Judging by the annoyed look on Joe's face, and the fact that he was keeping his lips pressed tightly together, I figured David had told his overspirit the same thing I'd told mine—not to talk to us while we were in school. Joe and Lao Lao immediately entered into a glaring match, as always, but this time they at least stayed silent.

"Ketchup and mustard." David shook his head. "You clearly need to brush up on your Chinese mythology, Winnie."

"Or maybe you need to brush up on your costume-making skills."

Ignoring that, David said, "I'm the Monkey King. Sun

Wukong. *Obviously.*" He puffed out his chest and stood up straight.

Ohhhhh. Sun Wukong. Right.

Sun Wukong, otherwise known as the Monkey King, is a famous trickster god in Chinese mythology. He was the star of a cartoon series that Lisa and I watched growing up, called *Journey to the West*. The title pretty much explains the whole plot of the series—the characters, a monk named Tang Seng and his disciples, journey to the west to fetch Buddhist scriptures. The mission sounds very simple, but it's made very difficult by the fact that demons keep trying to eat Tang Seng. Yeah, that's right. *Eat* him. Supposedly, Tang Seng's flesh has the power to grant immortality. In these kinds of stories, demons and evil people are always trying to live forever.

The character Sun Wukong has a really smart mouth, and an enormous ego to match it. The only reason Tang Seng even puts up with Sun Wukong is because the dude is *powerful.* So powerful that he once wreaked havoc on all of heaven, and nearly succeeded in bringing it down.

Point being, I didn't care what he said—David looked much more like a walking advertisement for ketchup and mustard than the mighty Monkey King.

"You really should get a refund for that costume," I said.

David glowered. "I didn't buy it. I made it myself from some old clothes I already had."

"Ohhhhh . . . yeah, on second thought, I can tell." I nodded.

"Hey, what's that supposed to mean?"

Fortunately, someone waltzed up to us, saving me from the need to respond to David. Unfortunately, that someone was Kelly. I didn't have any trouble figuring out her costume. She was dressed up as Minnie Mouse. On her head perched a headband with large black ears and a red bow, and she wore a black long-sleeved shirt paired with a red-and-white polka-dotted skirt.

When she was standing right in front of us, Kelly wrinkled her nose and stared at David. "Why did you dress up as ketchup and mustard?"

"I'm not dressed up as ketchup and mustard!" he groaned, smacking his hand on his forehead.

"Um . . . then what the heck are you supposed to be?" Kelly asked.

"David is the Monkey King," I informed her with a smirk. "Supposedly."

"Not *supposedly*! I most *definitely* am!"

Kelly snorted, unable to conceal a smile. We made eye contact, and I couldn't suppress my own grin. For a moment, laughing at David's failed costume, it felt like Kelly and I were on the same wavelength for the first time. For just a moment, it was like we'd reached an unspoken understanding.

Then Kelly's smile was replaced by her usual stony expression, and the moment passed.

"Don't forget what I said to you yesterday," Kelly said in a voice barely above a whisper. Her eyes darted around the room, as though she thought someone would be eavesdropping on us. But everyone was too preoccupied with the party to care what we were doing. "And don't worry about a thing, all right, rookie?" She gave me another smile, though this time there was no warmth in it. "Just enjoy your Halloween. Leave the protection of Groton to me."

I opened my mouth to retort, but found that I couldn't come up with anything brilliant to say in the heat of the moment. Or maybe it was because part of me wondered if Kelly *was* right. Were David and I better off leaving this peacekeeping business to her?

"We'll see about that," David fired back.

"Whatever you say, Mustard Man."

David turned bright red. "For the last time, I'm NOT MUSTARD!"

"What are you yelling about over there, David?" Mrs. Payton walked over toward us with a frown. Oops. "I hope you three aren't fighting today. We are, as you kids say, having *good vibes only* at this party."

We stared at her. The silence stretched until it became very, very awkward. Mrs. Payton had no idea that only old people trying to be cool would say something like that. And, honestly, it was kinder not to let her know.

"Well, that Kelly girl seems very charming," Joe said sardonically.

"Tell me about it," David groaned.

Despite the confusion over David's costume, Kelly being

rude as ever, and Mrs. Payton trying too hard to pretend she was young, there weren't any other mishaps at the class Halloween party. The almond chocolate chip cookies were a hit—the whole tray was gone faster than I could explain to people what I'd done: that I'd fused together Chinese and Western cookie recipes to make my own creation.

"Oo should shell dish food, Winnie," said Jeremy, his mouth still full of cookie crumbs.

I cringed. "Huh?"

"You should sell this food, Winnie," Jeremy repeated after he'd swallowed. There were streaks of chocolate around his lips.

"I'll pay *you* next time to finish chewing before you speak."

After we'd all gotten our food, Mrs. Payton put on a movie: *The Nightmare Before Christmas.* I also remembered watching it for Halloween in third or fourth grade. That movie seemed to be a classic that all the teachers loved, though I wasn't sure why. It was all right. The animation was kinda weird. I was too busy eating all the treats everyone else had brought in to pay attention to the movie.

If Lao Lao was right and there was some spirit nearby that was powerful enough to mask its presence from us, it was only a matter of time before something big happened.

As the morning passed with nothing strange stirring in or around school, I grew more on edge. Something was wrong. The day was going without a mishap. That wasn't right. That wasn't right at all. Even my most normal days didn't pass without mishaps. And today, Halloween, was supposed to be a very *not* normal day.

The rogue spirits were supposed to be attacking. That was what the Spirit Council had predicted; that was what Lao Lao and Joe had trained and prepared us for. The fact that I couldn't sense anything happening out of the ordinary was seriously freaking me out. No chills, no mysterious portals, no strange flowery smells, nothing.

Then, finally, something *did* go wrong.

CHAPTER EIGHTEEN

Toward the end of the school day, Kelly vanished. I wasn't sure exactly when she'd disappeared. It took until sixth period, Mrs. Walsh's algebra class, for me to realize that she wasn't in class any longer.

"Kelly Miao?" Silence. Mrs. Walsh looked up from her clipboard with a slight frown and scanned her eyes across the room. "Has anyone seen Kelly today?"

"She was in school earlier," said Tracy. "I saw her at lunch, too."

David, who was sitting all the way at the front of the classroom, turned around and raised his eyebrows at me. I had no idea what that meant. It could have been anything from *I think Kelly was kidnapped by the boogeyman* to *I have a wedgie.*

A cough sounded behind me. "Might I express my idea, Winnie?"

"Lao Lao, I told you not to talk to me unless it was an emergency. This is the second time," I whispered out of the corner of my mouth, as quietly as I could. Unfortunately it wasn't quiet enough. Allison turned in her seat and gave me a strange look. I just smiled at her. It must not have been a very pleasant smile, because Allison scooted her desk and chair away from me.

"My guess is that Kelly is in trouble," said my grandmother, proceeding as though nothing had happened. "She doesn't seem like the kind of girl who would just up and leave in the middle of school for no reason."

"Definitely not," I said, a little too loudly. A few of my classmates turned toward me. Oops.

"Is there a problem, Winnie?" said Mrs. Walsh. She paused in the middle of writing the agenda on the board and gave me a cold look.

My cheeks heated. "Um, n-no."

Then came a crackle over the loudspeaker. "Winnie Zeng, please report to my office," said Principal Anderson.

Uh-oh. That didn't sound good. A chorus of "oooooh" rose up from my classmates. "I didn't do it," I blurted, which I realized a split second too late made me seem even guiltier.

As I rose to my feet, I avoided everyone's gazes, my mind scrambling to try to figure out why I was getting called to the principal's office. I hadn't broken any rules or done anything wrong, as far as I was aware. Maybe I was being summoned for something good. But it wasn't like I'd done anything particularly good in school, either.

"I'll be back soon," I whispered to Lao Lao. "Stay here."

And despite my grandmother's protests, I sped out of the classroom toward the principal's office. The hallways were empty except for a couple of students going in and out of the bathrooms. Lockers were decorated with orange-and-black Halloween-themed cutouts, and a few classrooms had cobwebs and pumpkins outside them. Say what you want about Groton Middle School, but our Halloween spirit is on point.

My heartbeat raced faster and faster the closer I got to the principal's office. I couldn't shake off the dreadful feeling that something was terribly wrong. My gut feeling, my shaman sense, was telling me that I was drawing closer to danger.

"Um, hello?" I tentatively knocked on the door of the office, which had been left slightly ajar.

"Come in."

I opened the door and took a few nervous breaths. Principal Anderson was sitting behind her desk with her hands clasped together. She always looked stern, on account of the fact that she had curly gray hair, round glasses, and lips that I suspected were permanently pursed together in a thin line.

"You aren't in trouble, dear," said the principal with a small, grim smile that didn't reach her eyes.

"Oh." My shoulders slumped in relief—but only slightly. Something was amiss, though I couldn't quite pinpoint what. "Um, then why did you call me down here?"

Principal Anderson's eyes seemed a bit glazed and out of focus as she spoke. "Your father is here to pick you up from school, Winnie."

"Baba? He's here?" That was probably the last thing

I'd expected the principal to say. Surprised, I whipped my head around, but there was nobody else in the office—that I could see, at least. It was just me, Principal Anderson, and Principal Anderson's bookshelves and many potted plants.

"Hello, Winnie." That was a man's voice, eerily similar to Baba's, except deeper and strangely distorted.

Someone stepped out from behind Principal Anderson's chair. It was my father . . . but not quite my father. Baba's eyes weren't red like that, and he didn't have such big arm muscles. And besides, Baba smelled like his shaving cream. But as this figure stepped out into the open, a different scent hit me—the smell of flowers.

"You—you're not Baba," I stammered, backing away. My mind went foggy with panic. All I could think about was how I'd left Lao Lao behind in my classroom, and now I was pretty much defenseless.

Principal Anderson's expression had gone completely blank. She was no longer staring at me; she was staring through me. I wasn't sure what was going on, but my best guess was that she'd been hypnotized or was being otherwise controlled by this strange man—or spirit, or whatever it was.

The strange man smiled, and now I knew for sure this wasn't Baba. This didn't look like Baba's smile at all. This was a vicious smile, the smile of a predator homing in on its prey. "Clever girl," said the man. "I thought my disguise was very good, but you saw right through it."

"As if I'd fall for your tricks," I snapped. "Joke's on you, 'cause my father would never leave work to hang out at my school!"

The spirit seemed unbothered by my remarks. "You seemed to, as you put it, 'fall for my tricks' when I wore this disguise in your home."

Chills ran down my back as a terrifying realization struck me. Baba had been acting strange lately. What if that hadn't been Baba after all? What if that had been this spirit, pretending to be my father?

"I needed to keep tabs and gather information on you, little shaman," explained the spirit. "Also, I couldn't let you use the full extent of your powers for training, of course. I not only took on the form of your father—at times, I also took on the form of your charming older sister."

All of a sudden, everything clicked into place. Baba's and Lisa's strange behavior. Me struggling to produce even the most basic power. And the portal that had appeared at the Museum of Art History—was this the spirit that had escaped from it? It seemed more than likely.

"You," I spat. All those times I'd struggled to combine with Lao Lao, thinking that the fault lay within me. The whole time, this spirit had been messing with my powers, creating mental blocks. "You've been making training difficult for my overspirit and me! What exactly are you planning to do?"

"Don't worry, I won't hurt you—yet. First, let's see just how clever you are."

"Wh-what do you mean by that?"

A lopsided, frightening grin rose to the spirit's face. "Run along now, little shaman. I'll be with you momentarily."

Then the strange man vanished right before my eyes. I blinked, and when I opened my eyes again, he was still gone. I couldn't believe how fast that had all happened.

"What are you doing here, dear?" asked Principal Anderson, who was giving me a bemused look. "Did you need my assistance?"

"I . . . You called me down here," I said blankly, unable to think of what else to say. "Remember? And you said . . . you said my father . . . was here to pick me up."

"Your father?" repeated the principal. She sounded perplexed. "I'm sorry, I've never even met the man. Are you feeling all right, dear? Do you need to speak with the nurse?"

There was no time to waste trying to talk to the principal. Clearly, she had no recollection of what had just transpired. I thought quickly, trying to piece together what had happened in this office. The most likely explanation was that some evil spirit had taken on Baba's form and used its powers to put Principal Anderson under its control. Why had the spirit pretended to be Baba today, though? It seemed pointless, unless—

The realization hit me like a punch to the gut. The spirit must have lured me here to get me away from Lao Lao, get me away from my classmates—*in order to attack them.*

"I—I have to go."

"Winnie?"

Without further explanation, I turned on my heel and sprinted out the door, back down the halls. I was just in time to hear the final school bell ring. Students began pouring out of their classrooms. We were all supposed to now head down for a Halloween-themed school-wide assembly. Pushing past people, I moved as fast as I could toward my classroom.

When my homeroom was in sight, I spotted David near his locker. Quickly, I grabbed his arm. "David! Everyone's in danger!"

"What do you mean by that?" he demanded. "You left your backpack in the classroom, by the way. I grabbed it for you." He handed me my bag, and before I could thank him, he steamrolled on. "What took you so long in the principal's office? Did you actually get in trouble? Well, never mind. We're all supposed to go back to our homerooms now to head to the assembly."

"David, listen to me," I said before he could get another word in edgewise. The seriousness in my voice must have finally gotten him to pay attention to me, because he fell silent. "I—earlier, in the principal's office—I saw it. A spirit. I think it's the one I must have accidentally released when we were at the Museum of Art History."

David shook his head and raised a hand. "Wait, sorry, you're going way too fast. Come again?"

Impatiently, I explained to David what had happened. By the end of my explanation, all the blood had drained out of his cheeks, leaving them pale.

"But you don't know where this spirit disappeared to?" he said in an unnaturally high-pitched voice.

I shook my head.

"It has to be pretty powerful, if it's been pretending to be your family members, and also blocking your powers," David muttered.

"And it broke into the Department of Supernatural Record-Keeping and destroyed a bunch of records," I reminded him.

A bead of sweat trickled down David's forehead. He gulped. "Very, *very* powerful. Awesome," he squeaked. "Um . . . so what are we supposed to do now?"

"I don't know," I admitted. "I was thinking we should try to find Kelly first. If this spirit is really that powerful, we probably actually do need her help."

"But Kelly hasn't been in class for a few hours now," David said. "I was just thinking earlier that it's a bit strange how she randomly disappeared without a word to anyone, and . . ." Then a look of horror rose to his face. "Wait. You don't—you don't think she's been *kidnapped,* do you?"

Before I could reply, our Shaman Task Force badges lit up. David stopped in his tracks and gave me a wide-eyed look.

Thankfully the hall was wild enough with students and staff rushing about that we didn't have to worry about anyone overhearing anything they shouldn't, but unfortunately that also meant it was difficult to hear the Spirit Council through the badge.

"Agents? Can . . . hear me?"

"Yes, we can hear you," I practically shouted into the badge. "What is going on?"

". . . spirits . . . attacking . . . school . . ." The badge began crackling, as though there was a ton of interference. My frustration grew. The one time David and I really needed our badges to work, so that we could communicate with the Spirit Council during an emergency, of course they wouldn't be working.

But at least I'd been able to make out enough words to understand the gist of the Spirit Council's message. Spirits—as in plural, as in not just the one in Principal Anderson's office—were attacking here, now, at school. And it was up to David and me to protect them.

"Winnie! You need to stay here." Lao Lao came up over my shoulder. Her voice was filled with fear, and hearing that made *me* scared. I hadn't ever seen my grandmother this frightened before.

"They're here," said Joe in a hushed voice, floating up from behind David's shoulder. His eyes were wide. "They snuck into the school somehow. I couldn't sense them earlier—I don't know why—but now I can. They're *here*. I sense them in that direction." He pointed down the hall to our left, which was where the school auditorium was located.

Joe didn't need to elaborate on what he meant by *they*. David and I exchanged horrified looks. We knew exactly what he meant. The rogue spirits were here, in school. And now all the sixth, seventh, and eighth graders were about to file into one big room—where they'd be completely vulnerable.

It all made sense, in a terrible way. This had been planned. The school's Halloween assembly was the perfect time and place to harm a bunch of unsuspecting people at once. If I were a powerful evil spirit, I would choose to attack at that time to deal the most damage in an efficient manner.

"These spirits are way ahead of us," David hissed under his breath.

I reached into my locker toward the top shelf, where I'd put my ziplock bag of almond cookies.

"Is now the time to be snacking, Winnie?" David shouted.

I glared at him. "This food is the source of my power! Remember?"

"Oh. Right."

I shoved one, two, three almond cookies into my mouth, so quickly that I almost choked. It didn't help matters that almond cookies are, by nature, a bit dry. Within moments, a familiar warmth began spreading through my body, from my belly all the way to the tips of my fingers and toes. I was ready, or as ready as I could be. Judging by the determined expression on David's face, he was raring to face these spirits, too.

Now the question was—could David and I protect our school, and without Kelly's help?

CHAPTER NINETEEN

Instead of heading to homeroom first with the rest of the sixth graders, David and I followed a classroom of eighth graders who were already heading for the auditorium. It was easy enough to blend in with the crowd, since everyone was in costume. None of the students spared us a second look as we joined the back of the classroom line. The teacher was busy talking to another eighth-grade teacher as the group headed for the auditorium.

"So what's the plan?" David whispered to me.

I glanced around the auditorium. It was empty now except for the eighth-grade classes that had started trickling in, but I knew that within the next twenty minutes or so, the whole place was going to be filled with students and staff.

"We could ask the teachers to call off the Halloween assembly," David suggested, though his voice was filled with uncertainty.

"Yeah, right. And what will we tell them when they ask us why?"

"Um . . . the truth?"

"They'd never believe that spirits are real or that Groton is under attack." Adults never listen to kids, and they never believe that anything out of the ordinary could happen in real life. You'd think that with so many kids in books and movies getting into trouble because grown-ups don't believe them, the grown-ups in the real world would take notes or something, but no. Apparently eighteen is the cut-off age for having an imagination.

"It's too late for evacuation," Lao Lao agreed grimly. "Even if we did try to evacuate everyone, that would no doubt cause a panic, and the panic would only feed the chaos present in this school—which would mean feeding the evil spirits, making them even more powerful."

Joe added, "Our only choice is to try to find the spirits before they can launch an attack. And we must do so without raising any kind of panic or alarm, which would play right into their hands."

It was rare to see my grandmother and David's great-great-great-great-grandfather in agreement. Too bad it was because they were both gravely concerned about our current situation.

David and I had no choice but to follow the eighth-grade class we'd tagged along with, as the teacher led them toward the top of the auditorium. We sat at the very end of one of the rows, hunching over to stay as inconspicuous as possible. Then we waited as the classes continued to trickle in.

First the rest of the eighth graders came in, also sitting toward the back. Then the seventh-grade homerooms took the rows in front of the eighth graders. And finally I spotted the sixth graders coming into the auditorium, led by Mrs. Payton and Mr. Burnside. The noise level in the auditorium grew louder and louder, making it pretty impossible to try to pick out anything that could be a sign of trouble—a sign of evil spirits stirring.

"Where do you think the spirits are?" David murmured. He'd leaned forward in his seat and wore a look of pure concentration on his face as he stared down the rows at the stage. His left leg was bouncing up and down rapidly.

I shook my head. "No idea." I tried to clear my mind, as Lao Lao had taught me many times, to see if I could sense any spirits nearby. But there was no chill. It was almost as though the spirits had the ability to block us from sensing them. Maybe they did.

Then the microphone made a horrible screeching noise, causing everyone to groan. The principal was standing in front of the microphone in the middle of the stage. "Sorry, students. Ahem—shall we get started?" She glanced to the side curtain, as though awaiting someone's approval. Then Principal Anderson turned toward us and spread her arms. "Welcome, Groton Middle School, to the Halloween assembly! Today, we've invited the Michigan Majestic Magicians to perform a spectacular show for us in the spirit of this holiday celebration. A reminder of the behavior that I expect from each of you this afternoon . . ."

As the principal recited the standard assembly rules, I felt my attention drifting away from her. My eyes darted toward the sides of the auditorium. The teachers were standing at the ends of the rows where their students sat. There were a couple of custodians positioned toward the back. Other than that, nobody appeared to be out of place—and certainly, there was nobody present who looked like an evil spirit.

Where were these spirits hiding? What were they waiting for? They could leap out at any second, and David and I had to be prepared to fulfill our duties in a split second. Every seat in the auditorium was full, reminding me of what was at stake. My heart rate sped up.

". . . So, without further ado, please allow me to introduce to you: the Michigan Majestic Magicians!" finished Principal Anderson, and she walked off the stage.

Everyone clapped, and a group of four people wearing black capes stepped onto the stage in the principal's place. At that moment, David rocketed up from his seat.

"Th-that's them," he stammered, pointing at the stage.

The magicians raised their heads, and when I finally got a good look at their faces, I couldn't help it. I screamed.

CHAPTER TWENTY

That wasn't a group of people down there. That was a group of evil spirits, disguised as humans. Though they appeared at first glance to be humans, when I really stared at them, I realized their appearances kept flickering back and forth between human and demon. Their demon forms had green skin and horns.

No wonder we hadn't been able to spot any sign of trouble out in the audience. It was because the trouble was right there on the stage, hiding in plain sight. And the students and staff were *clapping*. They had no idea what was actually up onstage right now, no clue what was waiting in store for them. If they had known the truth, they'd have been screaming, not clapping.

"Hey, kids," said one of the spirits, in a scratchy, gravelly voice.

"Oh god oh god oh god oh god," David was muttering over and over to himself. He was shaking from panic, which only further freaked me out. "What do we do, Winnie?"

There wasn't time to think. I turned to Lao Lao. "We need to combine. Now."

Focusing all my efforts on concentration, I cleared my mind, as my grandmother had taught me, though it was exceptionally hard to do so now that my entire middle school was in danger. But maybe it was because my whole school was in danger that I *could* suddenly focus so well. Warmth traveled throughout my body, and then, as the heat grew and grew, Lao Lao's voice entered my head.

Can you hear me, Winnie?

Yes, I can hear you!

I glanced over at David to see that he, too, had combined with Joe, judging by the fact that Joe's spirit hovered over David's outline.

"Hey—what're you two doing over there?"

At long last, the nearby eighth graders seemed to have noticed that we were *not* their classmates at all. A handful of the nearest students gave us strange looks. I didn't know exactly what they were seeing, but judging by their expressions, whatever it was, it wasn't anything good.

"Um . . . bye!" With a wave, I leapt over to the staircase and began rushing down the stairs. David was hot on my heels.

"So what's the plan?" David shouted.

Thinking fast, I said, "One of us needs to get everyone out of here, and the other needs to distract the spirits. You go evacuate all the staff and students. I'll—I'll pelt the spirits with the almond cookies. That's the best I've got."

"Not the most sophisticated plan, but I guess it'll have

to do." Immediately, David turned on his heel and cupped his hands around his mouth. He bellowed, "EVERYONE, GET OUT OF THE AUDITORIUM!" He flapped his arms frantically toward the EXIT sign.

A few startled students glanced at us, then put their heads together to whisper. Nobody moved toward the door, but a teacher did start stomping toward us with a glower. "Hey! Which class are you kids from?"

Oh no. Our plan was already backfiring.

"Okay, time to improvise," I squeaked, grabbing David's arm. Quickly, we ran away from the angry teacher, toward the stage. "I guess we'll both have to just take down the spirits first!"

On the stage, the magicians had started their act. They had all pulled colorful ribbons out of their sleeves, apparently out of thin air. It was one of the oldest tricks in the book, but the crowd still went wild. In fact, the show seemed so typical that for a moment I thought maybe we were wildly mistaken, and we were about to go pelt a bunch of innocent human magicians with almond cookies.

But then the magician closest to stage left turned toward me, and I caught a glimpse of bared white fangs and glowing red eyes. No, these were definitely not humans. David and I sped toward them, past teachers who shouted after us, past rows of enthralled students. We sprinted until we reached the staircase that led up to the stage.

"Ah, it appears that we already have volunteers joining

us for this next act," said the nearest magician. The words nearly caused me to halt in my tracks. "Please give these two a warm welcome!"

The audience erupted into applause, which was not what I'd expected. The teachers were no longer even trying to stop us from running, and instead were giving us glowing, vapid smiles. In fact, it appeared as though *everyone* in the auditorium was smiling, but their smiles didn't have any substance to them. Their eyes were blank.

The nearest magician turned toward me, and I nearly screamed. Its glowing red eyes were a terrifying sight. Its fangs gleamed as black lips curled into a grin.

"On second thought, we don't need your help," the creature snarled. "We've already finished the act."

It snapped its fingers, and in an instant, a wave of motion followed in the audience. It took me a moment to register what had happened. Everyone had fallen asleep at the same time, as though they were under some kind of spell—a *real* magic spell. And I realized that they probably were.

"What did you do to everyone? Wake them up!" David shouted.

I didn't waste any breath yelling at the spirits. I grabbed a handful of almond cookies and was poised to throw them when one of the spirits turned to the others and said, "Our job here is done." Then it turned back to David and me with a sneer. "It's been fun, shamans, but we'll have to leave. We have a more powerful shaman to contend with—your little friend."

Little friend? My blood ran cold. The spirit could only be referring to one person—Kelly. Kelly, who had disappeared sometime in the middle of the school day.

What if she hadn't disappeared of her own will? What if she had been kidnapped by spirits? It seemed like the logical conclusion. But it was so hard to imagine Kelly in real trouble. She was so . . . powerful. She always had it together, and she'd proven that she was the best at whatever she did. It felt like things should be the other way around—like Kelly should be coming to rescue *me*. If Kelly was the one who needed rescuing, then we were in deep, deep trouble.

"Winnie—they're getting away!"

David's yell jolted me out of my thoughts, a fraction of a second too late. The four spirits turned on the spot and vanished in a puff of black smoke, leaving behind no trace that they'd even been here. Except, of course, for the auditorium full of sleeping staff and students.

Check on them, Lao Lao urged. *Quickly!*

I rushed off the stage to the nearest person, Mrs. Lee, who had fallen asleep leaning against the auditorium wall. I didn't know that much about checking pulses, but thankfully it was obvious that she was alive, just asleep. Mrs. Lee was breathing steadily, and she even snored a bit, too.

Once I'd checked my English teacher, I ran up and down the rows, checking a few random students to make sure they were all breathing.

"All clear," I shouted down to David. "They're just asleep."

"But the problem is they won't wake up," David replied.

He shook one of the students. The poor kid's arms flopped around a bit, but he stayed asleep.

I shook the shoulder of the nearest sleeping girl. "Hey. Wake up." But it was hopeless.

You won't be able to wake anyone until you've captured all the spirits responsible. Remember what Xiao Mao said to you before? Until every last evil spirit loose in Groton is returned to the department, the records fully restored, the spell upon this town and its people can't be broken, Lao Lao reminded me.

Of course I hadn't forgotten, but a teeny, tiny part of me had hoped that Xiao Mao was wrong and we'd only need to capture, like, 75 percent of the spirits. Or, even better, 25 percent. Twenty-five was a great number.

I should've known better. I never got to take the easy way out.

"We *need* to go after those spirits," I said to David. "We need to rescue Kelly, and we need to break this spell by defeating the spirits."

"I'll stay behind," David said.

I blinked. "What? Are you sure?"

"Yeah. Somebody's gotta look after all these sleeping people and make sure nothing happens to them—well, nothing else." David's expression was steely with determination.

Though I wanted to protest, David's words made sense. We couldn't leave all these students and teachers behind, at the mercy of another potential spirit attack. And even though David was a rookie like me, I'd seen him fight at his finest. I had to believe his power would be enough to protect everyone here. It *had* to be enough.

There was also a part of me that was nervous to seek out these evil spirits on my own. When I thought back to it, David had been by my side for pretty much every crucial battle. But David couldn't be with me now. I needed to track down the spirits' whereabouts and rescue Kelly—on my own.

You're not on your own, Lao Lao said. *You're with me.*

I nodded. "Okay. I'll leave it to you, then, David. Just call or text me if anything happens. I'll be back as soon as I can—with Kelly."

"You'd better be," David said.

With one last look at David, I raced out of the auditorium. It was time to put all my training to use.

CHAPTER TWENTY-ONE

Though it hadn't felt like that much time had passed in the auditorium, the scene that greeted me suggested otherwise.

The spell those spirits put on the auditorium likely affected the passage of time as well, Lao Lao explained.

Early evening had fallen in Groton, with the sun starting to dip below the trees. It was still light out, and the sun hadn't set yet, but I didn't give it more than an hour or two before sunset. It was chilly—not the spirit kind of chilly, but the fall weather kind of chilly—and I found myself wishing I'd brought a jacket to wear over my cat costume. Already trick-or-treaters were making their way down the streets in costume, holding bags for candy. They looked to be elementary-age, though I spotted a couple who were tall enough to be in high school. With a pang, I realized that all the middle schoolers were going to miss out on trick-or-treating this year, because they were currently all stuck in the auditorium under the spirits' spell.

But the trick-or-treating was the least of my concerns. If I didn't rescue Kelly and stop these spirits, there might be no future trick-or-treating, either. That alone was more than enough motivation for me to get going.

Though the evil spirits hadn't exactly shared their location with me, they didn't seem to be trying hard to conceal their whereabouts—judging by the huge cloud of green smoke that covered a building in the distance. City Hall.

Hurry! We don't have any time to waste, Lao Lao urged me.

"I know, I know." I wasn't exactly the fastest runner around—in fact, my mile-run time put me among the slowest at Groton Middle School—but it was different now when I took off at a sprint. Thanks to the combination of Lao Lao's powers with mine, I was practically flying.

"Hey, Mom! Was that the Flash running by just now?" shouted a small child in a bumblebee costume as I ran past him.

"Don't be silly, dear," said his mother in a distracted voice. "The Flash isn't real, and even if he was, he wouldn't come to boring old Groton, of all places."

"But I swear someone really fast ran by!"

"Now, Timothy, what did Mommy say about eating too much sugar . . ."

Poor kid was going to spend the rest of the evening trying to explain what he'd seen to his unbelieving mother. I raced down the streets, dodging and ducking and weaving past trick-or-treaters.

We need to come up with a plan, said Lao Lao.

The plan is to go inside, find Kelly, and then kick some spirit butt.

As soon as the thought left my mind, a group of screaming trick-or-treaters ran past. They couldn't have been older than five or six. It didn't take long for me to figure out who—or what—they were running away from.

A very beautiful black-haired woman wearing a flowy, elegant green gown was chasing the trick-or-treaters, laughing as though this were all part of a game. I might have thought her a normal, albeit stunning, human woman—if it weren't for the fact that when I blinked, she became a skeleton. When I looked again, shocked, she turned back into a human woman. But when I blinked yet again, she became a skeleton once more.

Definitely not a regular woman.

That's Baigujing, explained my grandmother. *A skeleton known for drawing people in with its lovely—and fake—human appearance. We mustn't fall for its tricks!*

"Help!" shouted one of the kids as he ran past.

This spirit really wasn't doing a good job of disguising itself if these little kids could see through it for what it was, but maybe it wasn't even bothering to hide its true self. Besides, kids were better at seeing the truth than adults anyway.

Let's go, Winnie, urged Lao Lao, but I was already way ahead of her. Reaching into my bag, I grabbed a couple of almond cookies and chucked them at Baigujing. One of the cookies missed, but the other hit its mark, landing on the spirit's cheek. *Yes.* The spirit hissed and backed away, reaching up a hand to pat the spot where it had been hit. When it lowered the hand, I caught sight of an angry red burn mark.

I grabbed two more almond cookies and was startled when Baigujing quickly snapped its head toward me, narrowing its skeletal eyes in fury. Okay, it was *really* scary when it looked at me like that.

Before I could move, the spirit lunged toward me with its skeletal hands. I wasn't quick enough to duck, and one of its bony fingers caught my hair, yanking it. I screamed, thought fast, and threw another almond cookie at it. This one sailed right into its eye socket, and now it was the spirit's turn to scream. It stumbled backward, raising bony fingers to its eye socket as though to soothe the pain.

You've got it now! Finish it off, Winnie!

But before I could move to obey my grandmother, the spirit merely laughed. Then it sped past me—right for the small group of trick-or-treaters, who hadn't gotten very far. I watched in horror as the spirit grabbed the two nearest children, one in each hand, and then took off in the direction of City Hall.

"Get back here!" I shouted, giving chase.

The spirit was fast, but I was fast as well thanks to the extra speed boost from Lao Lao. I sprinted down the street, following in the spirit's tracks.

As I turned the corner, there it rose before me: the tall, sleek gray building that was Groton's City Hall. Currently it was surrounded by that green smoke I'd spotted from a distance. Baigujing disappeared into the building. I ran through the parking lot toward the door, looking left and right, careful to be on guard for any spirit ambushes now that I was in their territory.

Winnie! Look out!

Almost faster than my brain could register Lao Lao's warning, I was surrounded. Hands with sharp nails grabbed my arms. "Hey! What the—" The words died in my throat as I looked up into the yellow eyes of a spirit. It had green skin, sharp yellow teeth, and a misshapen bald head. There were several others almost identical to it surrounding me.

"Shaman Task Force?" the nearest spirit read off my badge.

"Pathetic," scoffed the tall, slim one beside it. "Look at how puny and wimpy it is. They don't make shamans like they used to."

A couple of the spirits brought out a glowing rope, which they tied around Lao Lao. Though my grandmother shouted and kicked at them, they quickly had her arms and legs bound. I could do nothing but watch.

"Let go of me and my Lao Lao!" I didn't even care that the spirits had insulted me to my face; I was too busy panicking and trying to get out of this mess. The spirits cackled, and then put some golden duct tape over my grandmother's mouth, silencing her yells. But they didn't seem to realize that because we were combined, Lao Lao and I could still communicate with our thoughts.

I'm all right, Winnie, my grandmother reassured me. *Don't worry. We'll get out of this mess.*

I'll release you from those ropes as soon as I can! I promised.

I wriggled a handful of almond cookies out of the bag that I still clutched in my left hand, but one of the spirits knocked them out of my grip, laughing. I did manage to save a couple, though. Another spirit caught the bag, wound its arm like it was going to pitch a baseball, and chucked the rest of my almond cookies all the way over the roof of City Hall, into the trees.

Well, that wasn't good. My heart sank, and my stomach twisted with fear. Now I was out of options.

"You're coming with us," ordered the nearest spirit. "Don't struggle, or we'll make this painful for you."

The spirits pulled me toward the building, not bothering to be gentle. My mind raced as I tried to formulate an escape plan. At least they hadn't discovered my phone, which was in my back pocket. If all else failed, I could always call David for backup.

The spirits pushed open the doors to City Hall, and I gasped at the sight that awaited me.

CHAPTER TWENTY-TWO

There were a few more green-skinned spirits standing in front of the long table where the City Council members were usually seated. But I wasn't focusing on them. All my attention was concentrated on the evil spirit that sat front and center, where the mayor would normally sit, with a pot of tea on the table in front of it. The spirit was leaning back in the black leather chair as though it were a throne.

It was an evil spirit, more demonic in appearance than any I'd seen before—and that was saying something. The spirit had a bull-like face, with huge, gleaming horns beside its ears, and a large nose pierced with a golden ring. It had red skin rather than green, and a long, bushy red beard. From the shoulders and below, the spirit was built like an MMA fighter, with bulging arm and leg muscles. It looked way stronger and more powerful than any spirit I'd seen before. It clutched a fearsome weapon in its right hand— a golden spear with a wicked sharp, gleaming red blade. The spirit was wearing a brilliant golden robe—the same robe, I realized a split second later, that had been hanging in the glass display case in the Museum of Art History. The one that had vanished right before my eyes. My nose was overwhelmed with the scent of flowers.

This was definitely the spirit that had opened a portal to escape into the human world, bringing its minions with it.

I only knew one thing for sure—I did *not* want to get on this spirit's bad side. Though I guess I already was.

"Dà wáng," the spirits said, and then bowed to the red spirit. They forced me to my knees, too, even though I fought to stay standing.

King, translated Lao Lao. *This is their king. And he looks quite familiar....*

I'd seen enough Chinese cartoons that I'd recognized the phrase without Lao Lao's help. Though even if I hadn't, I could still have guessed that this spirit was their leader. It was always the biggest and most evil-looking dude.

"You may rise," said the king in a low, authoritative voice.

The voice. That was the voice of the spirit who'd taken on Baba's appearance. So he'd fled here after our encounter in the principal's office, probably commanding all the chaos at my school from afar. My hands curled into fists at my side.

I've just realized who that is, Lao Lao said. *This is the Bull Demon King.*

The title sounded familiar, but I couldn't remember where I'd heard it before. Judging by the sudden fear I sensed from Lao Lao, though, it definitely wasn't something good.

Do you remember the Bull Demon King from Journey to the West? Lao Lao prodded.

Ohhh. *Now* I recalled. According to the legends, the Bull Demon King had actually been a sworn brother to the Monkey King, but later became his sworn enemy. In fact, he was considered one of the main villains in *Journey to the West.* Which boded very well for us—not.

"Now, which one of you brewed this tea?" demanded the demon king with a scowl. "It tastes awful."

A terrified-looking green-skinned spirit slowly raised a trembling hand.

The Bull Demon King glared at the spirit. "How *dare* you feed your king such disgusting tea. It tastes like it expired a millennium ago."

"I'm s-s-sorr—"

But the spirit never was able to finish apologizing, because the demon king raised a hand. Eyes glowing, he shot a bolt of white energy out of his palm, which hit the spirit. The poor creature didn't have a chance. It was slammed back into the wall, and slumped to the floor in an unconscious heap.

The Bull Demon King turned his great yellow eyes on me, and it took every ounce of my determination not to let any of my fear show on my face. Even the other spirits looked terrified at their king's display of power.

"Hello again, Winnie," said the demon king with a twisted smile.

"You were the one who pretended to be my father in the

principal's office!" I accused. My heart was pounding, and my legs were trembling with anger. "And you've been pretending to be Lisa, too." A sudden realization struck me. "I thought it was weird that my sister's eyes were turning red, but that was you this morning!"

"And you ruined part of my plan because I overestimated your competence," growled the Bull Demon King. "I'd intended to infuse those cookies with magic so that anyone who consumed them would be compelled to obey me. Without that, I've had to improvise."

Good thing I hadn't made Lisa's cookies after all. Who knew that I'd end up saving people by *not* baking treats?

"You've got some nerve, trying to use me as part of your evil plan," I shouted, my fingers clenching into fists at my side.

"Don't get angry at me. Ask yourself why it was that easy for me to pretend to be your relatives and get close to you," the spirit said smugly. "All I had to do was study everyone's schedules, pick some convenient times when I knew they would be out, and impersonate them. It was almost *too* simple. The trickiest part was luring your sister away from her phone long enough to send you those text messages at your Chinese school." As the demon king spoke, I inwardly cursed myself for having played so easily into his hands. "That infernal Spirit Council really should screen shamans better before letting them into the Shaman Task Force."

That stung, because I couldn't help but think that the Bull Demon King was right on some level. Lao Lao had told me that I needed to focus on paying more attention to details, and now all the tiny details I hadn't stopped to question had cost me. I should have questioned Baba's strange behavior—coming home early, acting like he didn't know how to take off a jacket, leaving his phone behind. I should've thought harder about why Lisa didn't seem like herself at times, but I'd chalked it up to her exams. Plus, Lao Lao and I had suspected that there was some kind of spirit on the loose the entire time. I should have put two and two together much earlier than this.

It was terrifying to know that all along the demon had been sneaking into my home. That he could have harmed my family or me at any moment.

"My—my father and sister are okay, right? You haven't done anything to them, have you?"

The Bull Demon King snorted, the motion causing the golden ring in his large nose to sway. "No, you silly little girl. I haven't done anything to anyone . . . yet."

"And you're not going to do anything to anyone later, either!" I retorted.

The Bull Demon King acted like he couldn't hear me, though I did notice he had stopped his creepy grinning. He stroked his red beard. "That's not for you to decide. I've been planning my revenge for a long time—longer than you or even your parents have been alive, kid—and I intend to have it. I've already put the plan into motion. The first step was to reclaim my robe from the colonizers who *stole* it from me back in the Ming dynasty," sneered the demon king. He swung his robe around, letting it billow and shimmer in the air. "This robe contains the magic of deception, disguise, and interference, among others—it's far too powerful for those silly little mortals to display in their silly little museums. Now it's finally reunited with its *true* master."

As the Bull Demon King admired his robe, the pieces of the puzzle began clicking into place. That day at the museum, this spirit had escaped and taken back his long-lost golden robe. And everything that had happened since—my powers weakening, the spirit disguising itself as Baba—had been the Bull Demon King using his robe against me.

"Well, shaman, what do you think?" the Bull Demon King boomed, spreading out his arms in a gesture toward City Hall. "Doesn't this place look nicer than it did when those puny humans were running it?"

"Wh-where's Kelly? And the City Council members?" I blurted out. Nobody in Groton really liked the City Council members, on account of them always cutting school funding for useless construction projects, but that didn't mean they deserved to be harmed by evil spirits.

The Bull Demon King raised the spear and pointed toward the back left corner of the room. I hadn't noticed yet—the roomful of spirits had kept me pretty distracted—but there were a few people lying in a heap there, apparently unconscious. Spirits stood around and in front of them. I recognized a few of the humans, including Mayor

Greene and Kelly. Kelly was on her side, duct-taped and bound with glowing rope. Hovering above her was her overspirit, also bound with glowing rope.

My heart dropped into my stomach at the sight. Were we too late to rescue everyone? "What did you do to them?" I cried.

"Nothing." The demon king rolled his eyes. "They're just sleeping."

Relief flooded through me. "Kelly!" I shouted, rushing to her side. To my surprise, none of the evil spirits even attempted to block me, nor did they stop me from ripping the duct tape off her mouth.

"Ow!" Kelly winced and rubbed her lips.

"Sorry."

"Don't worry about it."

"What . . . What happened, Kelly? How did you get captured?" I asked. It was hard to believe that these spirits could have taken down Kelly. I'd seen her in action, and she seemed tough to defeat. I doubted that *I* could beat her if we ever battled for some reason. But then again, spirits possessed powers that I didn't.

Kelly lowered her gaze. "I was too brash. I overestimated my abilities. I . . . I feel bad, Winnie. It was arrogant of me, thinking I could protect Groton all on my own."

My eyes widened. Knowing Kelly, it was costing every last ounce of her pride to admit that she'd been wrong. Just realizing that caused the rest of my annoyance at Kelly to disappear. "It doesn't matter anymore. Now's not the time to be apologizing, anyway," I said. "Now's the time to kick some spirit butt!"

Kelly nodded, her eyes narrowed into slits of fury as she glanced past me toward the spirits. "Oh, I'm going to *destroy* these ghouls!"

"And how are you going to do that with your arms and legs tied up?" cackled one of the spirits near us, which had an unusually squashed nose.

"That's enough. Untie the shaman," ordered the Bull Demon King.

Squashed Nose startled and turned as though it had never seen its king before. "Wh . . . what?"

"I said, untie the shaman, you imbecile. Or do you not think we can handle one more puny shaman without using magic ropes?" sneered the Bull Demon King.

The spirit, clearly sensing the danger in answering the Bull Demon King's question, scurried over to Kelly without further protest. It was joined by one of its buddies. The two of them whispered something under their breath, too fast for me to catch—and in a language I couldn't recognize. They folded their hands and placed them under their chins. The ropes glowed brighter and then vanished.

Kelly jumped to her feet and then stumbled sideways. "Untie my Nai Nai too!" she shouted, pointing up toward her overspirit. Her grandmother was still bound by the glowing ropes, unmoving.

"And my Lao Lao!" I snapped. I glanced up toward Lao Lao and realized that her body had stopped moving. And suddenly I couldn't hear her thoughts, either.

Lao Lao? Are you there?

Silence.

"Ah yes, the special duct tape will have kicked in by now," said the Bull Demon King mildly, as though he were reporting the weather. "We won't be hearing a peep out of those pesky overspirits. Isn't that lovely?"

"Lovely? Put them back to normal!" I lunged upward, desperately trying to grab hold of the rope, but a spirit shoved me away from Lao Lao. I landed on my right side on the floor, trying to ignore the pain that shot up my arm and leg.

"Relax," said the Bull Demon King. "What's the rush, little shamans? Let's have a chat first."

"We can chat with our overspirits unbound!" Kelly threw back.

The demon king shook his head. "I fear you wouldn't be as open to a chat if your overspirits were unleashed. I'm not wrong, am I?" Kelly and I stayed silent, which seemed to be all the confirmation the Bull Demon King was looking for. "That's what I thought. Now, shamans, come here." He beckoned us to move closer to him.

Before I realized it, my feet were moving toward him. It took a moment for my brain to catch up to my body, and when it did, I stopped.

Oh no. My heart skipped a beat. Somehow, the Bull

Demon King could compel our bodies to move with his words. He really *was* more powerful than any other spirit we'd faced before.

"Ah, we've got a clever one here," said the demon king, though he sounded amused more than anything else.

"Whatever you're trying to do, it won't work," I snarled. "We're going to send you back to where you came from!"

The Bull Demon King blinked, and then grinned. With his great horns and beady eyes, the creepy grin made him look eviler than ever. "I think you're not quite understanding the gravity of your situation, shamans. Tonight is Halloween. It's *our* night. Isn't it, spirits?" He nodded around toward his spirit minions, and they all whooped and cheered. "Halloween is one of the times when we are at our strongest. And *you*, shamans and overspirits, made a big mistake by entering the territory that we've claimed as *ours*."

As the spirits laughed, Kelly turned toward me with a frantic glint in her eye. I'd never seen that look on her face before, and it made my stomach sink. Somehow I'd always expected that no matter what happened, Kelly would stay cool, calm, and collected. But now, with both of our overspirits tied up, neither of us knew what to do.

"Wait—where's David?" Kelly whispered, though I didn't think the spirits could hear us over their raucous laughter anyway.

"He stayed behind in the auditorium. Long story."

Kelly tilted her head to one side, eyebrows furrowed in confusion. But before she could press further, the doors banged open, the sound reverberating throughout the huge room.

"Dà wáng! We found the third brat!"

My heart flipped. Even before I turned around, I knew what I would see. And there he was: David, looking worse for the wear with mud on his face and clothes and a large red scratch on his forehead. Joe hovered above him, also bound in those glowing ropes.

"David!" I gasped.

"Hi," he said with a shameful little wave.

"What happened to you?" said Kelly, wrinkling her nose.

"I could ask you the same question," David shot back.

The spirit shoved him. David stumbled forward, nearly tripping onto his face. The Bull Demon King's minions had circled us, I realized too late. There was no escaping—not unless we tried to go through them. As we were all out-numbered *and* weaponless, with our overspirits bound, I didn't think we had great odds.

"So, shamans," boomed the Bull Demon King with a sneer, "would you like to hear my grand plan for the great city of Groton?"

CHAPTER TWENTY-THREE

"No thank you," I said, but the demon ignored me.

Of course the Bull Demon King had a master plan. Evil villains *always* have master plans. And they're never nice plans, either, like theme parks or universal basic income.

"I'd like to extend a generous offer, exclusive to you three shamans," started the demon king. He leaned forward. There was a glint in his eye, as though he were offering us something he knew we couldn't resist. "I like this little town of Groton, you see. It's small, it's out of the way— and most important, it contains an entrance into the spirit realm, which means it's the ideal place for spirits like us to gather. In fact, many have done just that."

"Yeah, we noticed," David muttered under his breath.

If the Bull Demon King heard, he didn't let on. Maybe he was too preoccupied enjoying the sound of his own voice. "My proposal is this: I take over Groton, and then slowly expand my power to the rest of the nation. You may have noticed already that my spirits are improving their skills of disguise and deception, hiding among the mortals," said the demon king smugly. "The three of you I'll appoint as my main lieutenants. You'll share the power evenly, and you'll be second in command in our new reign—after myself, of course."

So the Bull Demon King didn't really want to destroy us—he wanted to *recruit* us? This had to be the mother of all plot twists. I was struggling to wrap my head around the demon king's words as he continued.

"You'll take the lead in recruiting other shamans to the cause. And you'll even get to continue using your powers freely—in fact, I'd encourage it. Nothing makes a spirit more powerful than combining with a capable shaman. And nothing makes a shaman improve faster than combining with a hungry and powerful spirit. This would be a mutually beneficial arrangement, you see. And it would be such a shame to lose your power. What do you say?"

For a long moment, there was silence in the room. David stared at me, I stared at Kelly, and Kelly stared at the Bull Demon King with a wide-eyed, blank expression. Though I didn't think life could possibly get weirder, it just had. A demon king had proposed that we join up with him—and share his power. I mean, how was one even supposed to *respond* to that?

"Hey—but what about me, boss?" whined one of the spirits to the demon king's left. "You said if you ever conquered a sizable territory, you'd appoint me as your main—"

"You shut up and stay out of my way, Billy," snapped the Bull Demon King. The spirit shrank back and fell silent.

I couldn't believe the Bull Demon King's proposal, and

more than that, I couldn't believe that one of his evil hench-men was named Billy. It was absurd. Almost as absurd as an emperor named Joe.

"You—you want us to *join* you?" I asked, still processing the evil spirit's words. "But . . . we're shamans. We can only combine with overspirits."

"It's not that you shamans *can't* combine with us spirits. Traditionally, shamans and overspirits have joined forces, because for spirits, combining with shamans means giving them some of your power. Many spirits don't like that idea, because they can't see beyond their own greed," said Billy. "It's a weakness, if you ask me."

"Thank you kindly for explaining our weaknesses to the shamans, you utter buffoon," growled the demon king. The glower he gave Billy caused the poor spirit to shrink back, as he doubtlessly realized he'd made a grave mistake. He was definitely going to be punished after this.

Mentally, I filed away a note for later. "Our kind and your kind don't mix, though," I said. "That's, like, the first rule of . . . anything."

"Do I seem as though I'm the type to play by any kind of rules?" scoffed the Bull Demon King.

"He's got a point," David whispered.

"Rules are meant to be tested, broken, and rewritten. Join me, and I'll make sure you're always well-fed. You won't have to go to school. You can indulge in whatever activities you'd like. There will always be freedom, under my rule. What do you say? Come, now. You're children. You deserve to have fun and enjoy your youth, not serve that stuffy Spirit Council." The Bull Demon King spat out *Spirit Council* the same way some people said *week-old gym socks*.

For just a moment, I tried to imagine what kind of life that would be. No more homework. No more pain-in-the-butt group projects. No more torturously long piano recitals.

But if I dug deep down within myself, in my heart of hearts, I already knew exactly what to say and do. Yeah, maybe it would be nice to have more freedom, but I'd get sick of it quickly. Also, were these spirits going to cook me three square meals a day like my mom? I didn't think so.

"Didn't you say that you wished you had a father who had more time for you?" said the Bull Demon King, giving me a knowing look. "I could be that father figure for you."

My jaw dropped. "H-how did you know that?" I'd only spoken that thought out loud once before, when nobody had been around. Or so I'd thought.

"I have eyes and ears everywhere," the demon declared. Next he pointed a finger at David. "And you, boy. I know you wish your parents would hug you more. I could do that for you, easily."

David blushed. "As if I'd want *that*! A-and eavesdropping is rude!"

"It was far too easy to get close to you, too, boy," said the demon king.

"I knew Mom was acting strange," David burst out angrily. "You were impersonating her!"

"You should be thanking me. Didn't you enjoy those shrimp chips?"

As the Bull Demon King laughed, my mind circled back to something he'd said earlier. "How are we supposed to 'enjoy our youth' if you take over our town?" I demanded. "Yeah, Groton has its problems, and yeah, maybe nobody actually likes it here . . . but we like it a whole lot better than if a bunch of evil spirits were running the operations!" Probably.

"How do you know, if all you've ever known is rule by these musty humans?" countered the Bull Demon King. "Under my rule, you would be treated with proper respect, like the incredibly powerful beings that you are. You would be handsomely rewarded, spoiled with the most lavish feasts. You like candy? You wouldn't only be given heaps of candy on one day a year. It would be year-round."

"Our teeth would rot," David protested.

The Bull Demon King chuckled. "Silly boy, nobody would have rotted teeth, because there would be no dentists around to tell you that you do."

"That's flawed logic! Winnie, tell him . . . Winnie, are you *considering* this imbecile's proposal?"

I cleared my throat. "Of course not! Having no more dentists would be great—I mean, awful."

"Will everyone get this kind of treatment, or just us?" Kelly demanded. "Would you let our families and friends just suffer?"

The Bull Demon King rolled his eyes. "Nobody would

245

suffer. But those who aren't spirits or shamans—those without even an ounce of magical ability in their blood—would, of course, not lead the same glamorous lifestyles that we do. They are, after all, beneath us. Why do you think they celebrate *our* stories, pass them down from generation to generation? Stories about heroes and villains alike? It is because their respect and awe of our power is so great."

At that, my blood boiled. I couldn't believe that the demon king thought that evil spirits were better than humans. Not *all* humans were good—some could be quite as awful as the lowest of evil spirits—but this was the human world. And there was a reason the Spirit Council had stationed members of the Shaman Task Force all over the world, to keep the peace between our realm and the spirit realm. Spirits weren't meant to live here in the human world.

I opened my mouth to make a heated retort, but David let out a loud, fake cough and flashed his eyes at me.

"Um, we're going to take a moment to regroup and discuss your . . . your generous offer," said David with a forced smile at the demon king.

The Bull Demon King's eyebrows rose, but he made a magnanimous gesture with his left hand. "Go ahead."

David grabbed Kelly and me by the arm and pulled us toward the middle of the room, away from the table of evil spirits.

"David, what are you doing?" I hissed once we were out of earshot. "You're not seriously thinking of giving in to the demon king's demands? I get it, the no-dentists thing is tempting, but this is bigger than that."

"Yeah, that's like . . . not cool," Kelly added. "That's most definitely against the oath we swore when we joined the Shaman Task Force. We're supposed to protect humans to our dying breath."

David closed his eyes as though wrestling with something. I had a feeling I knew what. Before I'd known that the Bull Demon King had been impersonating Baba and Lisa, I'd thought it was nice that my father finally had a bit more time for me. Maybe David was feeling wistful about a mother who would hug him and let him eat junk food.

A few heartbeats later, David opened his eyes, and they were determined. "Of course I'm not considering the Bull Demon King's proposal. I'm buying us time," he whispered. "Do you two have so little faith in me?"

"Yes," Kelly and I responded in unison. Okay, I guessed we could agree once in a blue moon.

The Bull Demon King might have thought he'd swayed us to his side, promising to give us what we wished our families would. But he clearly didn't know anything about us. We would never let evil spirits take the place of our family members, much less all of Groton's population.

"I hate you both," David muttered. Then he shook his head. "Never mind. We need to go on the offensive right now. These spirits think they have the upper hand, so we need to attack while they're caught unaware."

Kelly let out a nervous little laugh. "Um, but they *do* have the upper hand. The spirits outnumber us, like, nine to one. And they came prepared to deal with us, too. They made sure we can't even use our overspirits." She glanced upward and then shook her head sadly. I followed her gaze. Lao Lao, Joe, and Kelly's Nai Nai were still trapped by the magical ropes.

"We can't call for backup, either," I said miserably, tapping the badge on my chest. "They've even interfered with our communication with the Spirit Council."

"They thought of everything," Kelly sighed. "These spirits are way cleverer than we gave them credit for. I . . ." She hung her head. "I know I definitely underestimated them. I thought I could take them all on my own, but clearly I can't." She gulped, gazing down at the floor in shame.

Though I was glad that Kelly was finally recognizing what I'd known all along—that the three of us needed to work together to take down these spirits—I couldn't help but feel a tiny twinge of annoyance, too. If she'd come to this conclusion earlier, maybe we could have handled all the spirits before Halloween, and they wouldn't have been able to infiltrate our school and City Council.

But pointing that out now would only be a waste of time. So instead I said, "There has to be something we can all do together to take them down. These spirits aren't invincible."

"Yeah, if the three of us combine our powers, we'll stand a chance. At the very least, we have to go down fighting," David said with a determined gleam in his eye. He held out his hand toward Kelly. After a moment, Kelly grabbed his hand and shook it.

As terrifying and hopeless as the situation seemed, David was right. Maybe there wasn't much we could do without full access to our overspirits. Maybe our best option was to put up a desperate fight and defeat as many evil spirits as possible before they took over Groton. Unless the Spirit Council was sending reinforcements that would arrive, like, now, I didn't see how we could win against so many opponents, even if we'd been training every day.

"Have you made a decision, shamans?" called the Bull Demon King.

I shot David and Kelly a terrified look. Neither of them looked particularly confident, either. David's forehead had broken out into a sweat, and Kelly's face had drained of color. But still, their eyes were clear with determination, and I knew that mine were, too. My heart hammered with fear—and the anticipation of a fight.

Maybe we did have one advantage after all. The fact that our enemies didn't expect us to even fight, the fact that we were willing to defend the human world at any cost.

"He thinks we'll back down," Kelly murmured, shooting the demon king a look. "Look at him, sitting all high and mighty in the mayor's chair."

"Maybe the Bull Demon King *does* expect us to put up a fight, but isn't even worried about it because he's that confident his forces will clobber us," David muttered.

I frowned. "Thank you for the vote of confidence, David."

"I'm just being realistic."

"Let's attack while we have the element of surprise on our side," I continued, as though David hadn't said anything. "That's our biggest advantage right now. I—I can go first. I'll tell the demon king that we're turning him down, and then we'll attack." Though I didn't know how much magic still remained in my veins, my insides were still reasonably warm from the almond cookies, and even without Lao Lao's help, I could probably clobber at least a couple of evil spirits with my bare hands.

"Ready?" I whispered. Kelly and David nodded. "Let's go."

Before I could chicken out, I turned around and walked as confidently as I could toward the Bull Demon King. I did my best to ignore the fact that my legs felt like jelly.

"We've made up our minds," I said.

The Bull Demon King cocked an eyebrow. "Oh?"

I nodded. "Yes." Steadying my voice, I said louder, "We refuse your offer."

Then, moving as one unit, the three of us rushed at the nearest evil spirits.

CHAPTER TWENTY-FOUR

As I'd predicted, we did have the element of surprise on our side. The first spirit I fought didn't even see my attack coming, thanks to my enhanced speed from the almond cookies I'd eaten earlier. I roundhouse-kicked it in the gut, which was enough to send the spirit crashing into the chair behind it, which then toppled another two spirits. In the process, they dropped their weapons. I snatched the nearest one—a spear—and leapt out of the way as a spirit sliced its sword through the air, right where my left arm had been a moment ago.

"This is just unnecessary," boomed the Bull Demon King. "You're going to lose this battle anyway; you might as well come peacefully. I implore you to reconsider. I'll even throw in a year's worth of complimentary bubble tea!"

"Complimentary bubble tea?" David repeated, pausing.

"Over our dead bodies!" shouted Kelly.

"Yes, that's the plan!" countered the king.

I didn't have the time—or breath—to waste trading barbs with the Bull Demon King. Right now it took all my focus to channel the remaining magic within my body. The evil spirits around me moved as though in slow motion, making it relatively easy for me to dodge their attacks and return their blows. My body moved almost before my brain could finish commanding it what to do. Lao Lao and I had trained together for so long that my body now knew the movements like the back of my own hand.

But then my limbs began to slow, as the magic in my system was slowly used up. Without the aid of almond cookies or combination with Lao Lao, I couldn't last more than one, maybe two minutes—not against so many opponents. Though I'd knocked down several evil spirits, more kept coming to take their place. Thinking about fighting against a great number of opponents was one thing. Actually going through with it was *totally* different.

A howl split my focus. Jolting in shock, I turned toward David. He was clutching his right arm, where there was a huge, bloody gash in his yellow shirt. The sword he'd been using clattered out of his right hand, and he fell to his knees on the floor.

"Capture him," said the Bull Demon King with a flick of his hand, as lazily as though he were ordering food.

"NO!" The scream ripped from my throat. Kelly was stumbling as she tried to get to David, but there were too many spirits still standing, and they swarmed her. I'd frozen for a bit too long, I realized in horror, as rough hands seized my spear and forced me down to the floor.

We'd lost. I'd known we'd lose, but the reality of facing

defeat was so much worse than I'd imagined. I desperately tried to lash out at the spirits, but my energy was leaving me quickly, until there was no more strength left in me.

Please, I thought as the spirits closed in, *Lao Lao, somebody, help.* But the glowing duct tape was still making it impossible for any of us to communicate with our overspirits.

Lao Lao. What if I never heard the sound of her voice again? What if I never heard Mama's and Baba's and Lisa's? It couldn't end like this. I wouldn't let it end like this.

". . . think we'll have to teach these shamans a lesson tonight," I heard the Bull Demon King say. "What do we think, spirits? We can start with the boy—before he passes out."

The spirits answered their king with a cheer. They were going to hurt David, then hurt Kelly, and then hurt me, if I didn't do something about it. And I *needed* to do something about it. These spirits couldn't be allowed to get away with so much chaos.

My frustration turned to anger. And then rage, like nothing I'd felt before, consumed me, as I lay there on the cold floor. With that rage came the voice that a moment ago I'd thought I'd never hear again.

Winnie?

Lao Lao! Relief swept through me, though the anger hadn't subsided. *How did you break through the duct tape?*

Everything was so dark, and I couldn't hear anything, and I couldn't speak. But eventually, you . . . I heard your voice. And somehow it gave me the strength to break free of those ropes. My grandmother's voice was filled with wonder.

I had no idea how I'd done that, but this wasn't the time nor place to ponder the extent of my abilities. *I need your help—right now.*

Let's show them what we're made of, child.

I was heating up, so much so that I didn't think it was possible for a human body to bear this much heat. With Lao Lao's guidance, I was no longer afraid—or at least my determination was much greater than my fear. Power pulsed throughout my body. I stood up quite easily, shoving aside the spirits like they were made out of nothing more than paper.

Glancing over toward Kelly, I could see that she'd managed to combine with her overspirit, too, and was now in the process of taking down all the spirits around her—with ease. Once she'd done so, she streaked across the room, so fast she was barely a blur of colors and movement, and grabbed something next to the still-sleeping City Council members. A large mason jar.

David was still kneeling on the floor, but he'd managed to combine with Joe. And a miracle was happening. The wound on his arm was healing right before my eyes, until there was nothing remaining except the crusted blood and the tear in his shirt to indicate that there had even been an injury.

As one, the three of us turned toward the Bull Demon King, our path cleared. The demon king's eyes were now wide with shock—and, unless I was mistaken, just a tinge of fear. Kelly raised the mason jar high above her head. She didn't need to explain her plan to David and me; there could only be one thing she meant to do.

Now I could see the True Name written on the Bull Demon King's forehead: *Du Jiao Gui Wang*.

Together, David, Kelly, and I chanted, "Evil spirit, no longer will you roam freely in this world. By the powers vested in me, I call you by your True Name and command you to return to your story. I name you—Du Jiao Gui Wang!"

With a cry, the Bull Demon King's outline grew bright, and then shrank.

"You haven't seen the last of me, pitiful shamans," bellowed the demon king, even as he continued to shrink. "Groton was only a small fragment of our master plan, and my masters will surely bring about terrible destruction. You don't even know what's coming, and once you figure it out, it'll be far, far too late. Mark my words!" The spirit's cackles grew quieter as he was sucked into Kelly's mason jar. The other spirits simply . . . vanished.

Those spirits are tied to the Bull Demon King's essence, explained Lao Lao, sensing my confusion. *Where he goes, they go. They're all soon to be banished back to the spirit realm.*

Relief swept through me, and then I found that I couldn't stand any longer, and I fell to the floor on my butt. Kelly and David followed suit. For a long moment, none of us said a word.

"What do you think the Bull Demon King meant there at the end?" David asked, sounding worried. "He said . . . he said '*our* master plan.' And I don't think he was just talking about himself in plural."

Kelly added, "And he mentioned something about his

masters. That means he isn't even the most powerful being involved in this plan. So who is the Bull Demon King taking orders from?"

"I don't know," I whispered. "It was weird that he tried so hard to recruit us to his cause, don't you think? Like, why not just get rid of us from the start? It almost seemed like . . . the Bull Demon King wanted to use our powers. But *why*?"

Kelly and David gave each other confused looks, and then shrugged at me. It was the first time I'd seen them so in sync.

"Maybe he just thought we'd be more useful to him alive than dead," Kelly suggested.

"Probably," David agreed.

Though Kelly's guess did make sense, I couldn't shake off the feeling that there was a more sinister motivation behind the Bull Demon King's wanting to team up with shamans. My gut was telling me that there was something we'd overlooked. But no matter how much I mulled over our exchanges with the Bull Demon King, I couldn't figure out what it could be.

"Winnie? You in there?" David waved his hand in front of my face. He peered at me in concern.

I blinked. "Oh, y-yeah, I'm fine. Um . . . we should get out of here."

We left, but the sense of foreboding followed me.

CHAPTER TWENTY-FIVE

Xiao Mao expressed an unusual amount of emotion when the three of us showed up, battered and bruised, at the front desk of the Department of Supernatural Record-Keeping. "Shamans!" Xiao Mao shouted. She placed a hand over her chest and shook her head. Her eyes were all big and shiny, like there were tears in them. "There you are. I've been worried."

I glanced around the department, noting how different it looked from the last time I'd been here, when it had been in a ransacked state. The books were arranged in neat rows on the bookshelves once more. The Paper Guard stood around the shelves, paper weapons out, ready to defend the department against any attacks. I wondered if they'd been punished for letting that spirit attack a week ago. There seemed to be more guards stationed here now than I remembered. But aside from that, nothing appeared out of the ordinary. If I hadn't seen the mess before, I wouldn't have known that the Department of Supernatural Record-Keeping had been attacked.

"You successfully completed your task, I take it?" Xiao Mao was saying.

"Of course," said Kelly. "I've never failed yet."

"*We.*" David sounded sour. "*We* haven't failed yet."

Our overspirits were all hovering near us, but they were fast asleep. I didn't blame them. The fight had sapped every last ounce of my energy. As soon as I got home, I was going to collapse in bed and sleep for a bazillion years.

But first, we still had an important matter to attend to.

I plunked the mason jar down on the desk. "Here. We've got this for you."

Xiao Mao reached for the jar with an apprehensive look. Then she took off her glasses, wiped them on her shirt, and peered intently at the swirling contents of the jar. Seemingly satisfied, she then began tapping away at her computer with her claws. "By the way, the Spirit Council has been pinging me all evening—they couldn't reach you!" Xiao Mao shouted so loudly that the overspirits woke up.

"Wus goin' on?" Joe muttered groggily. "We under attack again?"

"No, you paranoid geezer," snapped Lao Lao as she rubbed her eyes.

That insult seemed to wake Joe up pretty quickly. "*Geezer?* How dare you! That will be thirty lashes for you—"

"Oh, your days as emperor are long over. Wake up, you fool!"

Lao Lao and Joe continued throwing insults at one another, which meant life was back to normal.

"Are they always like this?" asked Kelly's grandmother, staring at the other two overspirits in alarm.

"Yeah," David sighed. He rubbed his temple like he was getting a headache. "Just ignore them."

Xiao Mao cleared her throat a little too loudly for it to be a natural cough. When we turned toward her, she prompted, "So, do you want to explain to me what happened earlier?"

Kelly, David, and I exchanged looks. Where were we even supposed to begin?

"Our badges malfunctioned," I explained, tapping my badge and frowning. "The spirit—the Bull Demon King—was too powerful."

"He created enough interference that we couldn't communicate with the Spirit Council," David added.

"I think we need badge upgrades," Kelly grumbled.

"You will be receiving those shortly," Xiao Mao said. "Now that you've saved Groton from an emergency, each of you will be promoted. The Spirit Council will see you now." She gestured back the way we'd come, toward the elevator.

Exchanging exhausted but excited looks, the three of us stepped into the elevator, our overspirits following close behind. Then we pressed the up button, and once the elevator arrived, made our way up to the eight hundred and eighty-eighth floor.

As far as I could tell, nothing had changed with the Spirit Council since I'd last been here. Had it really only been a matter of weeks since I'd come to be officially sworn in as a member of the Shaman Task Force?

We walked off the elevator onto clouds. Out of the clouds rose the twelve statues of the zodiac animals, which gleamed as though freshly polished. Though I'd been here before and knew the clouds were sturdy enough to hold our weight, part of me still couldn't help but fear that I might fall through them somehow.

"You'd think we would get a nicer reception, given how we saved the world and everything," David muttered. "At least a refreshment table or something. I'm starving."

"Shhhh. Don't be a brat," Kelly hushed him. That earned her a glower from David. Secretly, though, I had to agree with David. It wasn't like I'd expected the Spirit Council to roll out the red carpet for us . . . but if they did happen to have one on hand, now would have been the occasion to use it, just saying.

"Shamans," boomed a familiar, delighted voice. "Welcome."

It was Jizha, the leader of the Spirit Council. He emerged from behind the clouds, wearing his long gray robes. His white beard, which had been an impressive length when I'd first seen him, seemed to have grown even longer in the span of weeks. He was smiling so wide that there were crinkles under his eyes. When we approached him, Jizha clapped slowly. "Well done, all three of you. And a job well done by your overspirits as well." Jizha nodded at Lao Lao, Joe, and Kelly's Nai Nai, who bowed their heads politely back.

Around Jizha, the other Spirit Council members emerged from behind the twelve zodiac statues. All of them wore smiles and expressions of approval on their faces. Even Zhula, who'd given me a hard time when I'd joined the Shaman Task Force, gave us a begrudging nod. I thought there was even the tiniest trace of a smile on her face.

It was a nice change of pace to see so much appreciation in the council members' faces. Kelly was the first to kneel before the Spirit Council members. Quickly, David and I followed suit.

"By eliminating the threat of the Bull Demon King and restoring peace to Groton, you shamans have proven yourselves more than worthy of your respective titles," said Jizha. He spread his arms wide. "Because you aided the Spirit Council in an emergency task, the three of you are automatically promoted to the next agent level."

It took everything inside of me to not pump my fist in the air and shout, "Yes!"

"Kelly Miao—come forward, please." Jizha beckoned toward Kelly, and she stood and obeyed. "You're now a level two agent," he said, waving his arm toward Kelly's badge. The badge glowed brightly, and then turned a silver color. Kelly gazed down at the badge with a mixture of awe and wonder.

"David Zuo—come forward." David obeyed, and Jizha held out his arm toward him next. "Level one agent." After he spoke the words, David's badge turned a bronze color.

"And, finally, Winnie Zeng."

I got up from my knees and walked over to Jizha. I couldn't stop a smile from spreading across my face as Jizha said those magical words that I'd been wanting to hear.

"You're now a level one agent."

My badge lit up, turning from black to bronze. Lao Lao smiled at me, practically glowing with pride, and it was one of the best feelings in the world. I was grinning like a maniac, but I didn't care.

"Though peace has somewhat returned to Groton, that doesn't mean your jobs are done," Zhula sniffed. My smile faded. She always had a way of bringing everyone down. "The Bull Demon King's appearance in this town has proven that spirits are growing more powerful, able now to create unauthorized portals between the two worlds. We'll need you to be alert and prepared at any time for something similar to occur in the near future."

"Zhula, they've just completed a task," whispered Muzha. "Why don't we save the lecture for—"

"No, Zhula is right," said Jizha with a grim smile. "It's best that our agents remember to stay alert at all times. Evil could strike at a moment's notice. That being said, though, Winnie, David, and Kelly deserve praise for their achievements so far." He winked at us.

Though I probably should have left it at that, I couldn't

ignore the overwhelming urge to warn the Spirit Council about the demon king's parting words. "Um, there's something you all should know," I said, my voice shaking. I cleared my throat and did my best to steady my voice. The Spirit Council was a *really* intimidating crowd. "When we defeated the Bull Demon King, he said . . . he said something about '*our* master plan.' And he also mentioned something about his masters. I—I think he's collaborating with powerful spirits, even more powerful than he is. And he said we haven't seen the last of him, and that Groton was only a small part of the plan."

The council members immediately began murmuring to each other, wearing expressions of concern and alarm.

"Thank you for sharing that information with us, Winnie," Jizha said, inclining his head toward me. "That's helpful to know. We will, of course, be coordinating efforts with shamans across the country to strengthen protections against rogue spirits. In the meantime, you three should get a bit of rest. You've earned it."

Even though the meeting with the Spirit Council ended on a note that wasn't exactly triumphant, I left in a pretty good mood. I was a level one agent now. Me, Winnie Zeng. Reaching level one status hadn't taken too long after all, and getting to level two, I vowed to myself, was going to be even easier. I wasn't going to stop until I was all the way up to level five, and good luck to any evil spirits that got in my way.

None of us, shamans nor overspirits, were in much of a talking mood as we headed back down to the first floor of the Suntreader.

As we walked through the bookstore, waving casually at Mr. Stevens, Kelly broke the silence. "Well, I guess this is goodbye for now," she said once we were standing outside.

I stared at her, startled. "Why does that sound like you're going away?"

"Because I am. Now that my assignment in Groton has ended, I have to get back to Chicago."

"Like . . . *now* now? You aren't even going to say goodbye to our class?" David asked.

"Nah. Your classmates will forget I was ever here. The Spirit Council will make arrangements," Kelly explained. She flipped her hair over her shoulder, and then gave a rare smile. "I take back what I said about you two, by the way. Groton will be fine under your protection . . . probably."

"Probably?" David echoed indignantly. "Hey, Groton was always fine under our protection."

Kelly didn't even say anything, just raised her eyebrows at him and gave him an "oh, *really?*" kind of look.

"Mostly fine," David amended.

I couldn't believe it, but I thought I might actually miss Kelly, just a tiny bit. We hadn't started off on the right foot, but her direct personality and confidence had grown on me. I mean, Kelly never seemed uncertain of herself or scared of *anything*. She was so confident that she made others—well, me—feel like she could help turn around any situation. I couldn't tell her that, though. Kelly was already confident enough.

"Don't be too sad," Kelly said.

"Sad? Who? Where?" David scoffed, though I swear his eyes were a little teary.

"We'll meet again, pretty soon."

"We will, when the Spirit Council assigns *us* to help *you* in Chicago," I joked.

Kelly rolled her eyes. "Yeah, right. No, I'm talking about when the next Shaman Youth Tournament starts in the winter. I assume you'll both be attending, right?"

"Of course," I blustered, even though I didn't know when or where that would be, nor how to enter. But I remembered Lao Lao mentioning it a little while back. I'd have to ask her all about the Shaman Youth Tournament later.

"I'm going to win, of course," Kelly said smugly.

"Yeah, we'll see about that," David countered.

Kelly snorted, but there was a smile on her face. I even thought maybe she'd want a goodbye hug. But then she just stuck out her tongue and saluted us. Yeah, I guess a hug would've been too weird. Definitely not Kelly's style. "See you at the tournament, losers." Then she turned and quickly walked away, her overspirit trailing behind her, giving us a sleepy wave.

David and I stood there for several moments, watching

Kelly go, until she'd disappeared around the corner. He turned toward me, his eyes slightly watery. Maybe for once David was going to say something touching and nice to me.

"Well, now that Kelly's gone, looks like I'm back to being the best shaman in town," he said smugly.

I rolled my eyes and stood on his foot.

CHAPTER TWENTY-SIX

When I finally got home, I headed straight upstairs to go to bed. Not that much time had passed here in the human world—the passage of time in the Spirit Council defied all of Earth's laws—so nobody was home yet, though Mama would be within an hour or so. It was dinnertime, but I wasn't hungry. Trick-or-treaters would be arriving any time now, but I was too tired to go out or hand out candy. I fell asleep as soon as my head hit the pillow.

Unfortunately, I didn't get to stay asleep for very long. I was awakened by the sensation of someone shaking my shoulder, and none too gently.

"Winnie! *Winnie!*"

"Hrmmmmmph?" I rubbed my eyes, struggling to process what was happening. Lisa. My sister was all up in my face, shaking me like her life depended on me waking up. "Wh-what's going on?"

"I heard the *wildest* thing happened!" Lisa exclaimed. "There was a break-in at City Hall. Can you believe it? What kind of criminal tries to break into City Hall? Everyone knows there's nothing worth stealing there." She shook her head. "And no one's sure *exactly* what happened, but it seems like the magicians did something at the auditorium at the middle school! Did you see what happened? All my friends are talking about it."

Oh, right. As my brain slowly reawakened, I recalled how eventful Halloween had been, not just for me, but for everyone in Groton. It seemed like Lisa really wanted to hear the gossip firsthand from me. I bet the instant I told her my account, she was going to fire off a text to her friends.

"I, um, don't know exactly what happened at the school," I mumbled, which wasn't a total lie. Yeah, of course I remembered what had transpired, but most of it wasn't explainable—at least not if I didn't want to seem like I'd lost my mind.

"Really?" Lisa scrunched her nose. "Weren't you at the assembly?"

"Yeah, but . . . wait, was anyone from my school injured?" I asked. The sudden thought occurred to me as my brain woke up more. There had been too much chaos once we'd left Groton Middle School for City Hall. Though David, Kelly, and I had checked to make sure that the unconscious City Council members were fine before we headed to the Department of Supernatural Record-Keeping, we hadn't had the chance to make sure that everyone else was okay.

Lisa shook her head. "No. That's the strange part. It's like . . . these criminals, whoever they were and whatever they wanted to do, just disappeared into thin air. And once they were gone, everybody seemed to be fine. The criminals left a heck of a mess behind, though."

Well, technically they'd disappeared into a jar and were sent back into their storybooks, but I couldn't tell Lisa the truth for obvious reasons. She already thought I was weird enough.

I was just glad to see my sister was safe, and evidently none the wiser about the fact that the Bull Demon King had been impersonating her, which was probably for the best. Lisa would be *really* mad at me if she knew that I couldn't tell the difference between her and a demon.

"Are you okay?" Lisa stared at me, wide-eyed with concern.

"Um, mostly, yeah. Why?"

"When I heard something had happened at the middle school, I checked there, but nobody would let me in—that place is surrounded by police right now. So I came home, hoping to find you here."

I couldn't remember ever having seen my sister look so worried before. And definitely not over *me*. Not for the first time, I wished I could tell Lisa the truth of what was *really* going on. It would make both our lives a lot easier.

But I knew I couldn't be honest with her. Nor did I think she would believe me, anyway. Heck, if I were Lisa, I wouldn't believe me.

"Hey, so I was wondering, if you're feeling up to it . . . do you want to make cookies together?" Lisa blurted out of the blue. "Key Club extended the fundraiser to tomorrow because it was such a success."

Of course. Lisa's bake sale. I already knew about it, thanks to the Bull Demon King impersonating Lisa and asking me to make cookies, but Lisa herself didn't know that.

"I'd make them myself, but, you know, I'm not very . . . well, the last time I made cookies, I totally burned them," my sister admitted, her cheeks turning red.

"Making cookies is easy. If you want, I can teach you."

Lisa managed a small smile. "It's a little embarrassing, since I'm the older sister and everything. . . ."

I raised an eyebrow. "More embarrassing than it would be to bring store-bought cookies to the fundraiser?"

"Yeah, I'm *definitely* not doing that again."

Then the sound of the garage door opening filled the house. Mama was home. I glanced through the window toward the garage and was surprised to see a second car—Baba's black van—pulling into the garage. It wasn't even eight o'clock yet. Baba was home so early. Well, if it really *was* Baba, and not another evil spirit trying to attack Groton . . . but this time I was willing to bet that my father had come home. The Bull Demon King wouldn't be impersonating anyone for a while. Probably.

"We can make Mama and Baba help us bake the cookies, too," I suggested.

Lisa smiled. "Yeah. Let's do it."

I got out of my bed, and together Lisa and I headed down the stairs, where our parents were waiting.

"You're home early," Lisa blurted out.

"I asked for the afternoon off," Baba said. "I have been too busy lately." There was a guilty look on his face, and I wondered if he was feeling bad about how he'd forgotten about chaperoning my class field trip. That trip to the Museum of Art History felt like it had taken place ages ago. And I wasn't mad or even annoyed about it any longer. Too many things—much worse things—had happened between then and now. It seemed silly to hold a grudge over that. Plus, I was just glad that Baba was really Baba, and not some demon pretending to be my father.

"Well, since we're all at home, we can bake cookies together," Lisa said brightly. "Winnie's going to show us. Right?"

"I guess," I said with an exaggerated eye roll.

And I had to admit, the thought of my family all together for once, making cookies—it beat even the thought of trick-or-treating.

RECIPES FROM WINNIE ZENG'S COOKBOOK

Last time, I shared my prize-worthy mooncake and red bean brownie recipes with you. This time, it's almond cookies and egg tarts—*mmm!* You can make these for any occasion; the possibilities are endless. I've made them for a holiday party, a class bake sale, and even a celebration for that one time I beat David Zuo on a Chinese test. I once made egg tarts for Lisa, and she was nice to me for a whole *eight hours*. I'm telling you, these almond cookies and egg tarts will change your life. So what are you waiting for? You've *got* to try out these recipes.

Remember to always ask for a parent's or guardian's permission and supervision before you begin.

Happy baking!
—Winnie

Lao Lao's Almond Cookies

(Makes 16–20 cookies)

Ingredients:

1$1/2$ cups almond flour

Dash of salt

$1/2$ teaspoon baking soda

1 cup unsalted butter

1 cup white sugar (can substitute brown sugar)

2 eggs

2 teaspoons almond extract

Whole almonds

Optional: 1 packet of fortune

Directions:

In a mixing bowl, combine the almond flour, salt, and baking soda. In a separate mixing bowl, beat together the butter and sugar until creamy. Add one egg and the almond extract, beating them into the creamy mixture at low speed until well blended. Combine the contents of the two mixing bowls by gradually beating the flour mixture into the creamy mixture to form a dough, using a mixer or stirring with a spoon.

Flatten the dough and cover it in plastic wrap. Chill the dough in the refrigerator for approximately 1 hour.

Preheat the oven to 275°F. Line a baking sheet with parchment paper. Unwrap the dough and shape it into

1/2- to 1-inch balls, depending on desired cookie serving size. Flatten the dough balls so that they're shaped like coins before placing them about 1 to 2 inches apart on the baking sheet.

In a small mixing bowl, whisk the remaining egg. With a pastry brush or your finger, brush the egg on top of the cookies. Place a whole almond on top of each cookie and press down gently, about one-third of the way into the dough.

Bake the cookies for 25 to 30 minutes or until the edges are tan. Don't lose your patience like Winnie and eat them while they're piping hot! Once cooled, you can safely enjoy.

Mama's Egg Tarts

(Makes 16 tarts)

Ingredients for pastry dough:

$1/2$ cup water

1 egg, beaten

$11/3$ cups all-purpose flour

Dash of salt

$1/2$ cup unsalted butter

$1/4$ cup powdered sugar

16 aluminum egg tart molds (can substitute a muffin pan)

Ingredients for custard:

Dash of salt

$1/2$ cup white sugar

$1/2$ cup hot water

4 eggs, beaten

$1/4$ teaspoon vanilla extract

$1/3$ cup evaporated milk

Directions:

First, make the pastry dough. In a small mixing bowl, blend the water and egg until smooth. Then blend in the butter. In a large bowl, combine the flour, salt, and sugar. Add the wet and dry ingredients, mixing with a spoon or electric mixer until combined to form a dough.

Wrap the dough with plastic wrap and let it cool in the refrigerator for approximately 45 minutes.

Next, make the custard filling. In a large bowl, melt the salt and sugar with hot water, then let the mixture cool. Add the beaten eggs, vanilla extract, and evaporated milk. Stir until the ingredients are well combined. Cover this mixture with plastic wrap and let it cool in the refrigerator for at least an hour.

Preheat the oven to 400°F. Place the egg tart molds on a rimmed baking sheet. Spray them lightly with nonstick cooking spray. Remove the dough from the refrigerator and separate it into 16 pieces. Roll the pieces of dough into balls, and place one in each tart mold, pressing the dough against the bottom and sides. Remove the chilled custard filling from the refrigerator and pour the mixture into the dough shells until approximately three-quarters full.

Bake the egg tarts for 12 to 15 minutes, until the surface of the pastry turns golden. After removing the egg tarts from the oven, let them cool for approximately 20 minutes on a wire rack. Remove cooled tarts from the molds to serve. These treats are best eaten warm and with friends and family!

ACKNOWLEDGMENTS

Writing the second installment of Winnie Zeng's chaotic adventures wouldn't have been possible without some incredible people in my corner.

Many thanks to the entire team at Random House Children's Books who worked tirelessly on *Winnie Zeng Vanquishes a King*. Thank you to Caroline Abbey, Mallory Loehr, Jade Rector, April Ward, Megan Shortt, Barbara Bakowski, Rebecca Vitkus, Joey Ho, Kris Kam, Catherine O'Mara, Emily DuVal, Charlotte Office, Elizabeth Ward, and Nathan Kinney.

Thank you to my terrific editor, Tricia Lin! I will never stop gushing about your brilliance and passion for editing. I feel so very lucky that we get to work on Winnie's stories together.

Thank you so much to my agent, Penny Moore, to whom I dedicated this sequel. This is the seventh time I've gotten to write acknowledgments for a published novel, and it's thanks to you for helping me tell the stories of my heart.

Thank you to Sher Rill Ng for another stunning book cover.

To all the booksellers, educators, and middle-grade book enthusiasts whom I've been fortunate enough to encounter on social media and in real life—a massive thank-you for getting the Winnie Zeng series into the hands of young readers.

Without my readers, I would be lost. So, thank you to all the kids and lovers of middle grade everywhere for delving into the fictional worlds I've put to paper.

Last but not least, thank you to all the almond cookies and egg tarts I've consumed before, during, and after the writing of this book. Your sacrifices helped me push through to the finish line.